'Say your na ... **hissed at him** ... **with hatred.**

'My name is Shahin…Shahin of Zaddara.' Relief swept over him as he spoke the words. However much she hated him, and she did, for him this was the beginning of his journey to redemption. The tragedy of her parents' death couldn't be shut away any longer, and he had wanted to face it for so long.

The air crackled with tension as they stared at each other. It created a powerful energy between them—energy only he could defuse. He had to think on his feet, think how to keep her calm and get her to listen to him. At the same time he had to hide each one of the tumultuous feelings rising up in him, feelings driven by the fact that she was the only woman he wanted, the only woman he knew now that he could never have.

Susan Stephens was a professional singer before meeting her husband on the tiny Mediterranean island of Malta. In true Modern™ style they met on Monday, became engaged on Friday, and were married three months after that. Almost thirty years and three children later, they are still in love. (Susan does not advise her children to return home one day with a similar story, as she may not take the news with the same fortitude as her own mother!)

Susan had written several non-fiction books when fate took a hand. At a charity costume ball there was an after-dinner auction. One of the lots, 'Spend a Day with an Author', had been donated by Mills & Boon® author Penny Jordan. Susan's husband bought this lot, and Penny was to become not just a great friend but a wonderful mentor, who encouraged Susan to write romance.

Susan loves her family, her pets, her friends and her writing. She enjoys entertaining, travel and going to the theatre. She reads, cooks and plays the piano to relax, and can occasionally be found throwing herself off mountains on a pair of skis or galloping through the countryside. Visit Susan's website: www.susanstephens.net—she loves to hear from her readers all around the world!

BEDDED BY THE DESERT KING

BY
SUSAN STEPHENS

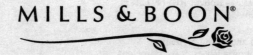

MILLS & BOON®

All the characters in this book have no existence outside the imagination of the author, and have no relation whatsoever to anyone bearing the same name or names. They are not even distantly inspired by any individual known or unknown to the author, and all the incidents are pure invention.

All Rights Reserved including the right of reproduction in whole or in part in any form. This edition is published by arrangement with Harlequin Enterprises II B.V. The text of this publication or any part thereof may not be reproduced or transmitted in any form or by any means, electronic or mechanical, including photocopying, recording, storage in an information retrieval system, or otherwise, without the written permission of the publisher.

This book is sold subject to the condition that it shall not, by way of trade or otherwise, be lent, resold, hired out or otherwise circulated without the prior consent of the publisher in any form of binding or cover other than that in which it is published and without a similar condition including this condition being imposed on the subsequent purchaser.

MILLS & BOON and MILLS & BOON with the Rose Device are registered trademarks of the publisher.

First published in Great Britain 2006
Harlequin Mills & Boon Limited,
Eton House, 18-24 Paradise Road, Richmond, Surrey TW9 1SR

© Susan Stephens 2006

ISBN-13: 978 0 263 84859 5
ISBN-10:   0 263 84859 0

Set in Times Roman 10½ on 12¾ pt
01-1106-48078

Printed and bound in Spain
by Litografia Rosés, S.A., Barcelona

BEDDED BY THE DESERT KING

CHAPTER ONE

SHE was tempted to take more shots, but her spine was tingling. And that wasn't a good sign when the man she had her camera focused on had a sidekick with a gun slung across his shoulder.

Zara guessed her target had to be one of the local tribal leaders touring the border of his land. But, whoever he was, he was magnificent. Capturing striking images was her stock-in-trade, though wildlife of a different kind had brought her to the wadi—rare desert gazelles and the Arabian oryx, graceful creatures that had been hunted to the point of extinction in some parts of the desert. They had been reintroduced into Zaddara in the early eighties and were said to drink here at dawn. The man was an unexpected bonus.

Zara tensed, realising he had started stripping off his clothes. The temptation to zoom in was irresistible. His torso was hard and tanned an even nutmeg and muscles bulged as he flexed his arms. Discarding his tunic, he let his trousers drop and she gasped as he stepped out of them, completely naked. It was a moment before she realised she hadn't taken a single shot. She made up for it now.

Wildlife photographer to hot-skin snapper? Zara smiled wryly. There was a whole world of opportunity opening up for her here. But she had no inclination to broaden her horizons in that direction even if she could use some of the images she was capturing now in the exhibition she intended to stage when she got back home... An exhibition that was supposed to contain more than wildlife images, Zara reminded herself. She had been hoping to capture something that would help her to forge a closer link with her late parents, not this incredible specimen...

Burrowing deeper into the sand hollow that served as her 'hide', Zara worked as fast as she could, hoping her camera lens wouldn't catch the sun and give her away. She had a living to earn, as well as a past to understand. And the truth about her past lay here somewhere in Zaddara...

Her parents had lost their lives in an oilfield disaster working as geologists for the late Sheikh. Sheikh Abdullah had been a simple man with a simple goal, and that had been to find oil to bring wealth to his impoverished country. Her parents had helped him to do that and had paid for it with their lives. The kingdom of Zaddara was now one of the major oil-producers in the world thanks to them, but the country had a new sheikh, and Sheikh Shahin was said to be far more ruthless than his father. Her late grandparents had always told her Shahin was responsible for the accident that had killed her parents.

Her jaw clenched as she thought about the blood money paid into her bank account each month. As soon as she was old enough, she had formed a trust to hold the money, then used it to fund the schemes she cared about. Recently she'd given a lump sum to a scheme that reintroduced rare species into their natural habitat. She refused to spend a penny of it on herself and had found solace of a sort from using the Zaddaran money to do some good.

Zara felt a shiver run through her a second time. It was a warning. Something wasn't right. Where had the bodyguard got to? Lowering the camera, she knew she shouldn't have allowed herself to become distracted. Capping her lens, she started to shuffle backwards down the slope towards her Jeep.

Shahin's jaw clenched with anger when he heard Aban's warning shout. He was poised on the edge of the wadi ready to dive in. He had waited almost a month for this promise of cool relief. He couldn't believe someone would dare to disturb his privacy now. He was in the middle of the desert. How far must he go to find solitude?

He had chosen the area for his retreat carefully. This place was at least fifty miles from the nearest habitation; only the Bedouin trails of his ancestors, hidden to those unfamiliar with the changing patterns of the desert, passed this way. There shouldn't have been a chance of him coming into contact with another human being. And now this…

Narrowing his eyes, Shahin shaded them against the first low-slanting rays of the sun. Staring up into the dunes, he could see two dark shapes silhouetted against the threatening red sky where there should only have been one. The area might be remote, but the fact that he hadn't checked their surroundings personally was a careless mistake. He could afford no more errors.

Casting another glance into the dunes, Shahin relaxed, seeing his bodyguard Aban had everything under control.

The intruder had been apprehended and it would dent the old man's pride if he were to interfere now. Aban was a good man and he would make sure he retired with honour. The elderly guard had travelled willingly into the wilderness with him to share the privations of a prince. A prince who had for a lifetime cared only for himself, and who must now be a king and father to his people. Only Aban knew the long days and nights of fasting were not just to prepare him to rule, but to drain the pus from a long-standing wound, a wound that even now could make him call out in his sleep and pound the sand with his fists in frustration that the past could not be changed. But if he must live with what he had done, he would learn from it. Diving into the freezing water, he powered across the wadi knowing that when he returned to the capital to be formally recognised by his people as the ruling sheikh of Zaddara he would take on all his father's responsibilities, however challenging. He was ready now.

Vaulting out of the water after his swim, Shahin grabbed the clean ankle-length *thawb* along with the flowing robe left for him by Aban. Adding a *howlis* to protect his head, neck and face from the harsh climate, he deftly fixed the long scarf-like head-covering in place.

A sharp breeze made him turn and in that moment he saw that Aban's captive was a young woman... Aban was holding her by the arm as they came down the dune together and she seemed none too pleased. Turning his face to the horizon, he shut her out. In his mind's eye all he could see now was the ruby-red glow enveloping the desert and the mountains in the far distance standing out in sharp black relief against a crimson sky. This was his land, a cruel land, and he loved it. He would allow nothing and no one to divert him from his chosen path.

The sound of the woman's voice intruded on his contemplation. Her voice was raised in anger and he resented the intrusion. Who was she? What did she want? Belting his robe, he turned to stare as the two figures approached. She was like a young colt walking awkwardly on the sand. Why was she alone in the desert? What type of person took such a risk? Was this journey into one of the most remote regions of the world worth so much to her?

His expression darkened when he saw how poorly she was equipped. Her outfit had no doubt been purchased from some fancy adventure-holiday equipment shop... But where was her survival gear? Where was her water canister? Where was her knife, her rope, her radio alarm...? Where were her flares? Didn't she know the first thing about the desert? Didn't she realise that a sandstorm could cut her off from her vehicle in seconds? Did she think she could snap her way out of trouble with that expensive-looking camera she was hanging on to so desperately?

As he strode towards them all these questions and more were beating a path to his eyes. But as the young woman raised a protective arm to her face he halted mid-stride. *Did she think he was going to hit her?* His expression was enough to make anyone think that, Shahin realised, standing stock still for a moment in silence. The breeze whipped up and took hold of his stark black robe, pressing it against his thighs, thighs that were still burning from his morning exercise. He saw her looking and felt his senses stir.

'Let her go.' He issued the command in a low voice,

but even though he had spoken in the throaty Zaddaran dialect she immediately caught his meaning and her face lit with anger.

'I should think so too!' Furiously she shook herself free from Aban's grasp.

As Aban moved to catch her again he was forced to make a fierce gesture to warn his faithful old servant to let her be. Such autocratic gestures didn't sit easily with him, but if he were to remain anonymous in front of this woman discretion was paramount. 'She's not going anywhere,' he observed, in English this time. 'Bring her to my tent…'

'What?' she exclaimed.

Her incredulity drew a faint smile to his lips as he walked away.

'Come back here!' she cried. 'Who do you think you are, telling me what to do?'

He had to stop, turn around and pacify Aban, before the old man made good the threat he made after this second outburst. It was fortunate for the young woman that she didn't understand the language! Grit, fire, courage, Shahin thought, noting the way she was glaring back at him. His curiosity deepened, but then Aban started to grumble again and, to defuse the situation, he was forced to point out that she was only armed with a camera.

Still muttering, the old man shook his head.

'Come with me.' He addressed her directly, gesturing towards his pavilion. The Bedouin blood running through his veins made hospitality mandatory however unpalatable that might be, and he had vowed to espouse all his father's values, not just cherry-pick them at will.

This time she made no protest. He was impressed by her

self-possession as she walked alongside him, though he could tell Aban was incensed by her easy manner. The old man thought no one should walk next to his king.

The old ways dictated that any guest must be welcomed to his tent for three days and three nights, which wasn't such a bad option in this instance. The young woman had obviously come to the desert seeking adventure—who was he to disappoint her?

As they drew close he could see that she wanted to take some shots of the Bedouin tent. He had to stop her before she went to work. 'No photographs,' he said firmly.

'What?' She didn't believe him at first, but quickly realised he was serious and left the camera to swing on the cord around her neck.

For the first time he had a chance to observe her properly and he could see that, beneath the layer of dirt and grime, she was quite beautiful. Her long hair, caught up in a casual ponytail, was the colour of creamy caramel. There was a hint of gold as well that the dust rising up from the sand couldn't hide…

Dust that had started to lift all around them, Shahin noted with concern. Staring out towards the horizon, he frowned. The red dawn sky had been an early warning of a storm blowing up. 'Move the Jeep to higher ground and stay with it,' he ordered Aban. 'The tents are secure, and I'll check them again before the weather worsens.'

Aban's smaller tent was pitched twenty yards or so from his own, but it was also beneath the same sheltering rocks. There was a third tent in the back of the off-road vehicle that Aban could use until it was safe for him to return.

Turning his attention back to the woman, he saw her

swallow with apprehension. She had caught the urgency in his words and he felt he should say something to reassure her. 'The weather is deteriorating, but you'll be safe here with me. Don't argue,' he warned, when she started to protest. 'You have no alternative but to stay. Aban tells me we have about an hour before the storm hits—and that's if we're lucky.'

'But it only took me two hours to get here from the city—'

Behind the defiance he saw her fear. 'That was before there were dangerous weather conditions to consider. You can't outrun the wind,' he pointed out.

He had no time to waste on persuasion and started off for the temporary structure that had been his home during his retreat, eager to check all the supports and ensure that they would withstand the force of the wind. To his surprise, she ran ahead of him and cut him off.

'If your man's leaving now, I want to leave too. We could travel in convoy—' Her chin tilted at a defiant angle as she held his gaze. 'And why don't you come with us? Why stay here if it's so dangerous?'

Because there were too many memories inside his tent, too many things that had belonged to his parents for him to risk losing them... The tent had been his father Abdullah's before he had claimed his kingdom. There wasn't time to dismantle it now, and so he would stay with it. But that wasn't her business. 'That just isn't possible,' he said coldly. 'And it's too risky for Aban to waste time trying to recover your Jeep. If Aban is to remain safe he must leave right away.' Veering away from her, he walked on.

She chased after him. 'But why can't I go with him?'

'Because Aban won't wait…' And because Aban's traditional values could only be stretched so far. He would be horrified were he to be asked to take charge of the young woman overnight. Aban wouldn't leave his vantage point until he was sure the storm had passed, and who knew how long that would take? He would not risk both their lives in order to appease this young woman's somewhat overdue sense of propriety. If she imagined that the desert was some big beach she was about to be cruelly disillusioned. The desert was a sleeping monster which, when awakened, had the power to destroy everything in its path. The only reason his Bedouin ancestors had chosen this site was because the surrounding rocks and fresh water offered them some protection. For now it was better not to alarm her. He didn't know how she would react if he told her the full extent of their plight. She might panic. She had no idea of the forces involved, or that everything around them was about to undergo the most radical change. He stopped and turned to gaze at the dune. 'Is your vehicle parked up behind that dune?'

'Yes, it is…'

She sounded hopeful and he guessed she thought he had changed his mind about letting her go.

'It's just over the hill, at the base of the dune.' There was a hint of impatience in her voice now.

'On low ground?'

'Of course, didn't I just say so?' Her irritation was mounting. 'I left it where it would be sheltered by the dune.'

'Sheltered by the dune?' A ghost of a smile touched his lips. She didn't have a clue. The storm that was about to hit them would have no respect for hills made out of sand.

'Leave it,' he instructed Aban, seeing the old man's glance swerve towards the dune. 'There's no time for you to climb up there and recover her vehicle. You must get yourself to safety and save our own Jeep.'

Zara wished she could understand the harsh, guttural language. She was way out of her depth. She wanted so badly to leave, but the leader of the two men was planted firmly in her way. Her options were limited. Both of these men walked easily on the sand, whereas the desert boots she had purchased in London gave her no stability at all on a surface she had discovered was as treacherous as ice. They would catch her before she made it to the base of the dune. And if she managed to escape, where would she go? If what this man had said about the storm proved to be right she would have to find shelter. As she gazed around, Zara could only try and visualise the thousands of miles of unseen land that rolled back behind the two men, hostile land with which she was unfamiliar. She had no alternative but to do as he said.

His tent was the size of a small marquee. As they drew closer Zara could see that the sides were made of some heavy woven fabric, which had been dyed a deep red. There was opulent fringing around a tented roof and the fabric was drawn up to a spike in the centre. Missing only a pennant, it reminded her of a medieval pavilion, reinforcing her opinion that she was stepping back in time, with a man who might be dangerous… A very attractive man who might be dangerous. Her heart was thundering—and for all the wrong reasons. She just had to keep telling herself that this was the photo opportunity of a lifetime…

But, as he raised the heavy curtain concealing the entrance to his tent, goose-bumps lifted on her arms. As she hesitated he tipped his chin, indicating that she should enter. The little she could see of his face beneath the folds of black cloth was hardly reassuring. His gaze was as dark and as unbending as iron.

'Come in,' he said impatiently. 'I have no intention of hurting you, if that's what you are worried about. In my country the safety of a guest is a sacred charge.'

Did that sacred charge extend to young women reckless enough to venture into the desert unaccompanied? Zara wondered. It must do, but she gathered from the hard look in his eyes that the prospect of her stay seemed nothing more than tiresome to him. He jerked his chin again and she got a sense of a man who was accustomed to having his smallest whim accommodated the instant he made it known. 'Dinosaur,' she muttered under her breath.

'What did you say?'

His voice had softened to the point where she had to strain to hear it and she shivered involuntarily to think that all his senses might be so keen. 'Nothing…'

His eyes challenged her assertion.

'Come in, or stay outside,' he said as if he couldn't have cared less what she did. 'Either way, I'm going in, and I'm closing down the entrance while I wait out the storm.'

'Are you threatening to leave me out here?'

'Take it any way you want.'

Firmly clenching her jaw, she walked past him into the tent. She saw him staring at her camera and clutched it closer. No way was he taking her camera from her. He might as well have tried to cut off her arm.

She was conscious immediately of the fresh, clean smell inside the tent and the neatness of it all. As she looked around, her eyes found their way back to her host. She noticed he wore a weapon tucked into his belt. She glanced at his face and back again. The long curving dagger looked lethal, but it had a beautifully worked gold hilt and she guessed it was more for ceremonial use than anything sinister. As her heart rate steadied she admired the intricate workmanship and longed to take a photograph of it so she could add it to the record of her trip. Perhaps if she asked politely she might persuade him to let her use her camera for some things in spite of his earlier objections. 'What do you call that?' she said, glancing at it again.

'A *khanjar.* Tradition demands that I wear it,' he explained, confirming her first impression. 'It is meant to represent a Bedouin's honour and is an indispensable piece of equipment in the desert. You never know when you might need a knife…' His dark gaze flashed up.

'Would you object if I take a picture of it?'

'Of the *khanjar,* no…'

The expression on his face left her in no doubt that her image must be confined to the dagger. She was careful to show him, as she narrowed her eyes in preparation for taking the shot, that the picture would be in close up and of the dagger and nothing else. She had no idea what else she might find inside the tent and was keen to respect his wishes in the hope of finding more material for her journal of the trip.

She had guts, he'd give her that. The dagger was beautiful and it pleased him to think she'd noticed it. It had been his father's and he felt Sheikh Abdullah's presence whenever he wore it. It both comforted him and served as a painful reminder that his work outside Zaddara had kept him away from a man he would have liked to know better. *And that now it was too late...* 'That's enough,' he said sharply, wheeling away from the probing lens.

His feelings of regret were not something he wished to share with this stranger.

She flinched at his impatience, but lowered the camera. 'This is what I do,' she explained with a shrug. 'It's all I do. I take pictures...wildlife, indigenous people, unusual rock formations—' She threw up her hands so the camera swung free on its cord around her neck. 'I don't know what you imagine, but I'm no threat to you.'

But was he a threat to her? Zara wondered. In the capital city of Zaddar women were equal to men, but here in the desert different rules applied. She could see that women would be bound by certain restrictions, strength being just one of them. If this man should decide to overpower her... She watched him releasing the bindings that protected the entrance to his tent. Once they were secured inside it, neither one of them would be leaving in a hurry.

It made her angry to think she had got herself into this position. She had researched the trip so thoroughly, reading everything she could lay her hands on, but nothing had prepared her for the vastness of the desert, or the emptiness. Compass, first aid kit, rug and a cold box full of supplies seemed woefully inadequate to her now. But Zaddara was supposed to be completely safe. How was she to know this man would send his armed guard to apprehend her? The thought irked her; his behaviour had been out of all proportion and she decided to challenge him about it. 'Was it really necessary to send a man with a gun after me?'

'I didn't send Aban after you; he took it upon himself to secure the dunes while I was swimming. Would you have me reproach him for doing his job so well?'

'The gun was unnecessary.'

'There are poisonous snakes in the desert,' he countered, 'if you had bothered to check.'

She *had* checked. What sort of amateur did he take her for? But she drew the line at carrying a gun. A camera was her weapon of choice, and she used that and the images it produced to challenge the motives of the people who killed the creatures she had made it her life's work to protect. 'Nevertheless—'

'Nevertheless?'

The rejoinder came back sharp as a whip crack. And it was a mistake to hold his gaze. Having never had her blood pressure raised by a man was no preparation for an encounter like this. The Bedouin was unlike any man she had met before. She could usually judge people from their appearance, but this man was an enigma. Tall and powerfully built, he was tanned a deep bronze and his steely eyes were watchful. He had brought her inside his tent only because he had to. She sensed he was a deeply private man who didn't want her there any more than she wanted to take the risk of being alone with him.

'It was wrong of you to travel so deep into the desert without a companion—'

'I didn't have a companion to bring—' Zara's mouth slammed shut. Why had she admitted to being alone? 'People know I'm here, of course.'

'Of course,' he agreed in a way that suggested he didn't believe her for a moment.

Following him deeper inside, she looked around. As she had first thought, everything was spotlessly clean and orderly and was made comfortable with heaps of intricately embroidered cushions and finely woven rugs. In a variety of rich colours, these were perfectly arranged in piles to relax and recline on. A slender coffee pot made from what looked like beaten silver rested on a simple brazier and the delicious smell made her swallow involuntarily.

'You are thirsty?'

He had barely any accent at all, she realised now, and the rich baritone strummed something deep inside her. Coffee was a good starting point if she was going to strike up a dialogue with him and get to know more about his land and customs. 'I'd love a coffee, thank you…'

How many people got the chance to see inside a real Bedouin tent and find out how a man like this lived? Zara wondered as she moved past him to sit on the cushions he indicated. He made her feel tiny and delicate, which she knew was survival of the species at work. However hard she might try to fight it, her female genes craved his masculinity—and she wasn't fighting nearly hard enough.

The lanterns hanging from the main frame of the temporary structure cast a soft light over the tent's interior and there was another lamp in one corner by what looked like a bed. She inhaled the faint scent of sandalwood appreciatively and found the warmth reassuringly cosy after almost freezing to death on the dunes.

When he offered her a dainty coffee cup full of dark, steaming liquid she was careful not to touch his hand. Taking it, she sipped cautiously. The delicious taste reminded her of rich dark chocolate. She drained it to the dregs.

'More?' he invited.

As he spoke he was unwinding the coils of protective headgear. Zara watched in fascination as a head of hair, thick, black and glossy was revealed. She had to wonder what it would feel like beneath her hands. Jet-black curls caressed his neck and some of the waves had fallen over his forehead so that the hair caught on his lashes. He was an incredible-looking man and the expression in his eyes was both compelling and dangerous; it took all she'd got to look away.

As he refilled her coffee cup and their eyes met she saw a world of experience reflected in his gaze. She found a face so strong it frightened her arousing? Maybe that was because his lips in contrast to his fierce expression were lush and curved with sensual beauty. He was considerably older than she was, perhaps thirty-five, and it only made him seem all the more desirable. Back home she would have been blushing by now and would have looked away, but here the situation was so unreal she felt no such restrictions and stared back boldly.

She had read that the Zaddaran Bedouins were so close to the earth, so in tune with the planet, that they never travelled aimlessly but returned each year to the same locations, using the stars to guide them as well as stone markers they left behind them on a previous trail. They could tell from the few shrubs in the desert when it had last rained and how much rain had fallen, and could find water, recognising by sight and smell whether it was toxic or brackish or safe to drink. What did this man know about her? Anything was possible. As she sipped the hot, dark liquid in her cup a dangerous fantasy swept over her where his strong arms had claimed her, and his fierce, sensual mouth…

'More coffee?'

'Yes, please…' She started out of the reverie with relief. This wasn't a story to which she could dictate some fuzzy romantic ending. She was here with an older man from a very different culture who, fortunately for her, was bound by centuries of tradition that demanded he treat her well. That was the only reason she was here drinking coffee with him, and that was why she would have to leave the very first chance she got.

'Would you care for a bath?'

'A bath?' Zara's mouth fell open as he gestured towards the rear of the tent.

'Another custom…' His eyes were shaded. 'Water is the greatest luxury we have to offer our guests in the desert.'

What he said made sense, but was she running the risk that he was simply adding ever more fantastic 'traditions' to his list?

'Aban heated the water for me before he left. You would be quite private behind that curtain, and I'm sure I could find you a clean robe to wear…'

Zara glanced down. She was extremely grubby. It had been a long drive and then a long wait to capture the images she wanted in the freezing desert dawn. She was still chilled through and uncomfortably gritty in all the wrong places, but that was no reason to behave rashly. 'That's very kind of you, but I couldn't possibly—'

'Why not?'

'Well, I…' She floundered for a moment. 'I don't even know your name.'

He made the typical Arabian salutation, touching his forehead and then his chest in what she thought was a slightly mocking gesture.

'I am a simple Bedouin.'

Which was true, Shahin reflected. All Bedouin were equal according to their custom. Leaders of his people were chosen for their wisdom and judgement, as well as their ability to tread a wary path amidst a society peopled by hard, ambitious men. 'As bathing is considered a great luxury in the desert,' he went on, 'and is one of our most cherished traditions, it would be considered an insult to refuse…'

Maybe that was stretching it a bit, but his bath *was* going to waste. And maybe he had resented her intrusion to begin with, but she was mature and self-possessed in a way he suspected very few people in her situation would be. And now she was here…

'Your tradition?' Zara racked her brain, but she was certain she had read nothing about baths being offered to guests of the Bedouin. She would have been surprised if she had. If water were so precious they would hardly waste it on bathing. But if this man were a tribal leader, perhaps he had his own set of rules. 'You mean this is a tradition of your tribe?'

'My tribe…?' He leaned back so she couldn't see his expression in the shadows.

'I understand if it is…' And then another thought occurred to her. 'But surely your traditions don't prevent you from telling me your name?'

She might be young, but she was shrewd, and he would have to handle her with care. 'My name is unimportant.' He made a closing gesture with his hands.

'To me, it is important. I have to call you something.'

He could hardly believe she was still harassing him. 'You may call me Abbas—' The name flew from his lips before caution could stop him. Abbas had been his mother's name for him. 'It means lion,' he started to explain.

'Of the desert?' she interrupted him lightly. Then, seeing his expression, she dropped her gaze.

But he was under no illusion that she was frightened of him. She wasn't afraid of him, except in a primitive way like any woman who knew a man wanted her in his bed. She feared his masculinity, but she wanted her share of it. She feared him as a man, not as a leader of men. The realisation made him harden instantly. 'The water is warm,' he murmured persuasively.

'And scented with sandalwood?'

He inclined his head.

CHAPTER TWO

Yes, all right, this was crazy, Zara fired back at her inner voice. Sinking deeper beneath the scented water naked while her Bedouin was only a few yards away behind a curtain… She would never, *never* behave like this under normal circumstances. But she had been so grubby and uncomfortable, and his promise of fresh warm water on a day when nothing was normal had tipped the balance. Trouble was, she could talk it through inwardly all she liked but that didn't stop her heart racing out of control.

'Are you all right in there?'

Zara hurtled upright at the sound of the deep male voice. The chance she was taking seemed a whole lot bigger suddenly. 'Yes, thank you, I'm fine…' Her voice sounded strained. And where were the clothes he'd promised? What was she supposed to do now? How long could she reasonably remain submerged in rapidly cooling bathwater? Was this Abbas's idea of a joke? Or was he preparing her for—? She gasped as a hand appeared around the curtain.

'Here are a couple of towels for you…'

'Thank you…' She could hear another voice now…

Zara tensed, listening. It was an older man! What on earth had she got herself into?

Springing out of the bath, she seized the towels and flung them around her, securing them firmly. Once she was decent, she put her ear to the curtain, which was all that divided her from the two men. They were talking in the husky Zaddaran dialect and she could tell little from their tone of voice.

'Here…'

She started back as Abbas's bronzed hand appeared around the curtain holding some sort of flimsy robe.

'Well, take it…' he instructed impatiently.

'What is it?'

'Something for you to wear?' he suggested bitingly.

Zara watched in fascination as the hand stretched out a little more, revealing a wrist shaded with dark hair. Having located the wooden stand, he let the robe fall over it.

'And here's a veil to go with it…'

Having disappeared again behind the curtain, the hand came back and this time she got a good look at the powerful forearm attached to it… A robe and a veil? What did Abbas think this was—his harem?

'You'll need some fresh clothes,' he pointed out, anticipating her concern. 'Unless you're going to come out of there wrapped in towels, of course.'

'Thank you…' The robe was lovely…pure silk, Zara found on closer inspection. In the softest shade of sky-blue, it was heavily embroidered with the tiniest silver cross-stitch she had ever seen. The matching veil was as light as air, the merest wisp of silk chiffon in the same delicate shade…

'Get dressed quickly,' Abbas instructed. 'I have allowed a man to shelter inside Aban's tent until the storm has passed. I don't want you scaring him half to death—'

'Me?'

'Yes, you… The man's a silk trader, hence your new robe, but the sight of you wearing it would alarm him. Women in the desert usually have more discretion and never appear in public dressed in such a manner.'

But it was all right for Abbas to see her dressed like this? Even as her hackles rose, Zara felt a twinge of guilt. Perhaps it was the only robe the trader had that was suitable and Abbas needn't have troubled to buy it for her. Glancing at her travel-worn clothes lying crumpled on the floor, she realised how grateful she was to have something clean to wear, especially something new and so undeniably feminine… But her doubts returned the moment she slipped her feet into the dainty jewelled mules Abbas had just pushed under the curtain. She had taken a bath in a man's tent in the middle of a desert—a powerful hunk of a man she didn't even know, and now she was wearing a seductive outfit of his choice.

'Do the mules fit? I took a guess at the size of your feet.'

'It was a very good guess.' And if he knew her shoe size, what else had come under his close scrutiny? Zara wondered.

'Are you ever coming out of there?'

Abbas's impatience sent a little shiver of awareness rushing through her. Pressing the robe to her body, she was just checking to see if it was transparent when he spoke again.

'May I?'

Making a last pass with her hands down the front of the robe to make sure she was decent, she straightened up. 'Of course…'

He flung the curtain back.

'Our fashions suit you…'

'It's very kind of you to say so…'

'Not kind at all—a simple fact,' Abbas assured her.

Closing her eyes, Zara inhaled the faint scent of sandalwood and tried not to imagine what could happen in these sumptuous surroundings with her authoritative, seductive host. She thought about the easy command he had over his words, his actions, his body…

What would it be like when they were making love?

Zara banished that thought immediately, conscious that Abbas was still waiting for her. 'I'll just sponge these clothes down and then I'll be right with you,' she assured him briskly. She might be dressed for seduction, but the practical side of her nature always won through. She was keen for him to be aware of that. Pushing the silk chiffon up her arms, she got to work.

She would have to keep a tight rein on her thoughts, Zara reflected, hanging her clothes carefully over the stand to dry out. All these fantasies about harems and seduction were dangerous. Combing through her hair with her fingers, she adjusted the robe so that it hung properly and tried the veil. With the veil on it felt like dressing up—different, fun, glamorous… 'What shall I do about the water in the bath?'

Did he think she was going to leave that for Aban to deal with too? Zara wondered as she came to join Abbas in the tent. Hunkered down by the brazier, he was putting fresh coffee grounds into the pot. As he stared up in frank admiration their gazes clashed, which brought fresh streams of sensation rushing through her veins. She had to let the veil slip in order to clutch the robe a little closer. Shouldn't he look away now? Zara wondered, feeling her cheeks flame. To distract from her discomfort she attacked him on another front. 'I'm surprised you'd allow Aban to carry up water from the wadi just so you could bathe.'

'*I* brought every drop of water up from the wadi. Aban is my man, not my slave.'

She couldn't help but feel a small glow of appreciation at his words. Or maybe the glow had started when she stared at his lips—they were such sensuous lips.

'You have beautiful hair,' Abbas observed softly.

Zara was suddenly conscious of the weight of her waist-length hair and its silky lustre. It felt soft to her touch and the brush of it against her cheek had never felt so sensuous. Even the way it fell into natural waves when it had been washed, which had always annoyed her in the past, seemed suddenly an advantage. She had never thought of herself as beautiful before.

Abbas made her feel beautiful, Zara realised, wrinkling her brow in confusion. She was relieved when he turned away at last. It gave her a chance to study him covertly. But now the glow she had felt moments before raged into an inferno. Heavily shaded with dark stubble, his face was the hardest face she had ever seen…and she just knew that his body, concealed beneath the flowing folds of his robe, would be the body of a fighting man, hard and beautiful.

'I'm going to shave,' he said, picking up a knife. 'Why don't you sit by the brazier and dry your hair while I'm gone?'

'Gone?' She didn't want him gone…not with a storm threatening outside.

'I won't be long—'

'Fine…' She tilted her chin at a confident angle, but something in her voice made him turn to reassure her.

'I'll secure the tent before I leave. You'll be quite safe.'

A fierce gust of wind made the decision for her. 'I'm coming with you.' She grabbed her camera.

'No, stay here and dry your hair—'

'I like to dry my hair outside.'

'Where the air is full of sand? And you don't want sand in your camera, do you?'

Clean out of reasonable excuses, Zara sank down on the cushions again. It was getting progressively darker inside the tent—another indicator that forces were at work over which she had no control. According to Abbas, she wasn't safe outside and she didn't feel safe inside. She was his prisoner as surely as if she were locked inside a cell. And somehow she had to subdue the *frisson* of excitement that provoked.

'Stay here—where you'll be safe,' he repeated as a parting shot.

Did she want to be safe with Abbas?

Reduced to drumming her fingers on the hide couch, Zara was longing to pick up her camera. But she had given Abbas her word. She would ask his permission before taking any more photographs. It was only fair when he was sheltering her from the storm. She couldn't betray his trust. Her heart lurched when he walked back inside the tent and she saw his gaze flick to the camera. It was still in its case just as she had left it. The approval in his eyes sent fire racing through her veins, but even a shave couldn't soften the hard planes of his rugged face. His cheekbones seemed more pronounced than ever, his jaw stronger.

'What are you worrying about?' His brow creased.

'Worried? I'm not worried.' She met his gaze levelly, but the expression in Abbas's eyes added a dangerous spark to the scent of hard, clean man.

She watched him seal the entrance with strong, capable hands. A few robust tugs and he appeared to be satisfied that everything was secure. He moved on around the tent, checking the supports and ignoring her. She should be pleased about that, Zara told herself. The wind had picked up and sand was hitting the sides with an ominous hissing sound. When the tent poles groaned beneath the pressure she began to get worried.

'Are you sure it's safe?' She had to yell to make herself heard above the noise.

'I'm sure—'

'And Aban? Do you think he will have reached safety by now?'

Abbas looked pleased that she had remembered. 'Yes, I checked on him while I was out.' Pulling a satellite phone out of his pocket, he tossed it on to the bed.

She could have rung for help. Why hadn't she thought of it before? 'Could I borrow your phone?' Her mobile was still in the Jeep.

'There's too much static for a call to get through now.'

She hid her disappointment. 'How about the trader?'

'He's safe too—'

And then, before Abbas could say any more to her, a juddering blast made her exclaim with fright.

'Don't worry.' Abbas ran his hand down the ballooning sides of the pavilion. 'This dense fabric is made from camel hair. There's nothing better for keeping out the weather.

And these supporting poles may look flimsy, but they flex to accommodate the force of the gale just like the trunk of a palm tree.' Wrapping his fist around one, he caressed it.

'How long do you think we'll be here?'

'It's impossible to know, so you might as well relax and get used to your confinement…'

Relax? That was easy for Abbas to say—her bones were turning to liquid fire at the thought of being secured inside the tent with him and her heart was vibrating frantically, though not from fear.

'Well, I'm going to relax even if you won't…'

'What are you doing?' Zara stared, unbelieving, as Abbas calmly began shrugging off his robe.

'Getting undressed…' His voice was casual.

'Put your clothes back on again. Now,' Zara ordered hoarsely. Abbas stalked about naked when he was relaxed? Beneath his Zaddaran dignity Abbas possessed an elemental quality that both frightened and excited her. She hadn't got the measure of him and that frightened her too. And now he was testing her she was sure of it. She could lose her mask, tell him the truth—that she was more innocent than she seemed, that life had made her act a lot older than her age, or she could play it cool.

She was relieved when she didn't have to make that choice. Having loosened his robe, Abbas stretched out on a bed of hides and closed his eyes. All she could see now was a glimpse of hard, tanned flesh above the topmost folds of his robe, though where it fell away she could see the loose-fitting trousers he wore beneath…trousers slung low enough to do more than hint at the toned athletic body underneath.

Sucking in a deep, shuddering breath, Zara was almost ready to believe she could feel the warmth of Abbas's naked flesh reaching out to her—warm, fragrant, sandalwood-scented flesh that she longed to feel pressed up hard against her own. Shifting awkwardly on the couch, she knew she was slipping into an even deeper state of arousal. The thought of easing that frustration had crossed her mind… Everything was so unreal—like a day out of time… A day when she could allow herself to be seduced by a man for whom she felt an overwhelming attraction… To have Abbas make love to her… One night of passion with the lion of the desert… And who would know? She was sure Abbas would know everything there was to know about pleasing a woman.

Zara's breathing grew more ragged as she developed her fantasy… A man she didn't know—an older man, an experienced man, a man whose eyes promised exotic pleasures beyond her understanding, a man whose lips she longed to feel all over her body, even those secret places no other man had seen…

But Abbas was a man of principle. He had already proved that by his care for Aban and the trader. There was no way he would touch her while he was treating her as an honoured guest. The best thing to do was to act calmly and normally, as he was doing, and push the dangerous fantasies from her mind.

Reaching into her bag, she drew out a pencil. 'Would you mind telling me what each item of clothing you're wearing is called? I want to be sure I get everything right when I prepare my journal back home.'

Opening one eye, Abbas turned to look at her. An expression of faint amusement flickered across his face, but then he shrugged and, resting his head back on crossed arms, he started to talk.

While her heart hammered away, Zara took refuge in her professional eye. The decoration on his robe was a testament to the skill of the local needle-workers. The gold thread picked up the amber lights in his eyes, something that added to his attraction, and she hadn't noticed before. The dramatic contrast of that and the black fabric of the main body of the robe was a perfect foil for his black hair and for his dark skin tone as well as for his strong white teeth… She could almost imagine them nipping into her flesh…

'Do you have a problem?'

Zara realised she had stopped writing and was gazing into space with a dreamy look on her face. 'No, no, I'm fine.' She drew herself up. 'It's really interesting…' She smiled to encourage him to keep on talking, while she indulged in her fantasy—her nice, *safe* fantasy.

'Perhaps when you return to the city you will buy some eastern clothes to remind you of your time in the desert?' Abbas suggested.

'I'm sure I shall…'

'Though you're more than welcome to keep the robe you're wearing now—with my compliments.'

'This one? I couldn't possibly.' Zara's gaze flew over the intricate workmanship. She guessed the silk robe must have cost a fortune.

'Don't you like it?'

'I love it, but—'

'But?' Abbas pressed. 'You don't accept gifts from

strangers?' he guessed shrewdly. 'So what if I sell it to you? Would you take it home with you then?'

She didn't want to go home yet… And, as for selling the robe to her… Zara's heart lurched as Abbas's lips curved in a way she hadn't seen them do before and her heart stormed into overdrive as she considered the price he might have in mind. 'Do you accept travellers' cheques?'

'I'm a little short of banking facilities, as you can see…' He laughed softly. 'But you could owe me…'

'I'm not sure I'm comfortable with that…' She stood up as she spoke.

'Where are you going?' He sat up.

She had to get away. She had to take a moment to cool down. 'To look outside—'

Springing up, Abbas stood in her way. 'No…'

'No?' She looked at him, and then down at his hand on her arm.

His dark eyes flared, but he spoke softly as he lifted his hand away. 'If you move that curtain the sand will come flying in. The entrance cover must remain as it is until I say it can be opened.'

'So I'm a prisoner here?' Turning away from him, Zara could feel the tension mounting.

'You're here as my guest,' Abbas reminded her.

She could feel him behind her and her pulse responded eagerly to the remorseless beat of his virility. Abbas had thrown an erotic noose around her, which he then pulled tight. 'Let me go,' she warned in a whisper, hardly realising that he wasn't even touching her.

'Or you'll…what?'

She could feel the sweep of his breath across the back

of her neck and had to fight not to tremble. She didn't start breathing again until he stepped away and felt as weak as a puppet when the strings had been let go. And had left her more aroused than ever.

Abbas understood everything about tension—tightening and releasing the invisible cord until it was she who was being driven to make the first move. The blood in her veins had turned to molten honey. Caught in the ambit of Abbas's darkening stare, Zara had to wonder how long she could hold out if it came to it. Abbas was so hard, so elemental, and his robes left so little and yet too much of his powerful frame to the imagination. Rampantly masculine, he was a natural-born hunter... Was she really ready to take him on? And then there was her own lack of experience where sex was concerned to consider... She would almost certainly disappoint him. The elements chose just that moment to intervene. While she was hesitating, the wind gave a terrible roar and, shocked into action, she launched herself into Abbas's arms.

'Sorry—' Gasping with shock, Zara made as if to pull away, but Abbas held on to her. It was a hold so gentle that if she had wanted to she could have broken free at any time...

'Please,' he murmured, brushing her hair with his lips. 'Don't apologise, Adara...'

'Adara?' She raised her eyes to look at him.

Placing one finger over her mouth, Abbas dragged it slowly down over the full swell of her bottom lip as if to remind her how aroused she was... And to tell her that he knew. 'I will call you Adara...'

It meant virgin in his language, but she couldn't know that. It pleased his sense of irony to call her by this name.

Though she was young she had the assurance of a much older woman. His Adara knew what she wanted, and she knew he could give it to her. There would be no complications; she was on the same wavelength he was, and it amused him to see how she squared up to him even now. Her face was flushed and he had to wonder how much of that passion would be channelled into their lovemaking. Nothing was a foregone conclusion and he liked that about her. She was cool and self-possessed, but she could be defiant too and he had never encountered disobedience before. Her unpredictability fuelled his appetite, and would certainly stave off boredom while they waited out the storm.

She collected herself quickly, as he had expected, and he was ready for her. As she went to move away to take her seat on the couch again he made sure their fingers brushed—as if by accident. Her swift intake of breath told him everything he needed to know. And as the moment froze he held her gaze.

CHAPTER THREE

'The storm is easing…'

As Abbas spoke, Zara watched him move towards the entrance as if the sexual temperature between them had never flickered. Maybe it hadn't for him. Keenly aware of the progress of the storm outside the tent, maybe he was oblivious to the storm he had whipped up inside it. Or was he toying with her? Which one was it?

'If the weather is improving I want to leave as soon as I can…'

'Three days and three nights,' he said, turning to face her.

So he had remembered. 'Your custom?' She raised a brow, wanting him to know she wasn't convinced.

'Custom demands that, having sought refuge here, you must remain as my guest for three days and three nights…' His face told her nothing as he sat down again and arranged his robe around his legs.

'You're serious, aren't you?' She had to drag her gaze away and ignore the heavy throb of anticipation in her lower body.

Raising his head, Abbas levelled a stare on her face. 'I am bound by the customs of my land…'

'But I am not.' It was too shadowy to interpret his expression with any confidence, but Abbas's silence suggested she was mistaken. She didn't press him, knowing he would probably reply that at this moment she was a guest in his land.

Zara found it hard to relax. Abbas's commanding manner had aroused her to the degree where his slightest move made her heart race. He made her long for things that had never mattered to her before, forbidden things. She hardly dared to imagine what it might be like to be held by him, to be cradled in his arms, to be touched delicately, persuasively… As he leaned forward to check the coffee she saw the flare of recognition in his eyes and pulled herself round. 'As soon as the trader leaves, I'm going with him. Even if my Jeep has been lost, it doesn't matter. I'll hitch a lift with him.'

'On his camel? And I think you'll find that he has already gone.'

'But the storm has only just died down…'

'Come with me, Adara…'

When Abbas released the entrance cover Zara uttered a sharp breath of amazement. The desert was peaceful again, but they might have been carried up and brought down in a totally different place. What had happened to the dune where she had been captured, the dune behind which she had sheltered her off-road vehicle? Now all she could see was a flat plain that stretched away into the distance as far as the foothills of the mountains. The sand around the tent had formed into wavelike ripples. The structure was now isolated in a vast expanse of flat featureless nothingness, like a ship floating on a sea of sand…

Looking further, Zara was relieved to see that at least the palm trees clustering round the wadi had survived. But they were bent at such an acute angle their fronds were brushing the water... She found it much easier to walk in the flat sandals Abbas had provided and was suddenly eager to escape the confines of the tent. Hurrying over to the nearest palm, she touched its trunk gently with her hand. 'Will it recover?' She glanced at Abbas, who had come to stand by her shoulder.

'Yes,' he reassured her. 'The trunks of the palm are as flexible as the poles used to support the tent and so they will recover, given time.'

Leaving her, he strode towards the second tent, which had also survived the onslaught of the storm. Picking up her skirts, Zara hurried after him.

There was no sign of the trader or his camel. There was nothing to show that he had been there at all other than a bundle hanging from the fronds of a palm. 'What is it?' Shading her eyes, she looked up into the branches.

'I have already told you that hospitality is instilled at birth in the Bedouin, and so is repayment of the debt.'

Was Abbas sending her a hidden message? Zara wondered, pressing him to continue.

'That cache will contain whatever the trader can safely spare. It is his way of thanking me. But I am honour bound not to touch anything I don't need, the point being I must consider the needs of others over myself.'

His words sent a shiver tracking her spine. 'Perhaps I could copy some prints to send to you when I get home... I have taken some good landscapes...' As she gestured around, Zara felt her offer wasn't enough. 'And I'll send you a cheque too, of course.' She couldn't bear freeloaders and didn't want Abbas mistaking her for one.

'A cheque?'

'Money for the time I've spent here as your guest…'

'I do know what a cheque is. I just wondered why you should feel it necessary to send one to me.'

'To cover the cost of sheltering me, of course,' she said, frowning.

'Are you always so scrupulous?'

'Yes.' She held his gaze steadily. 'I never use people and then just walk away.'

'But you haven't left yet,' he pointed out, 'and I may need to add something to your account.'

Zara's eyes widened. She didn't know whether to believe Abbas or not.

He couldn't resist provoking her just a little more. Three days and nights… It was an outrageous idea, even if he had based his assertion on ancient lore. Traditions such as that had never been meant to apply to a situation like this. But he could hardly blame his ancestors for not factoring into their thinking one reckless young female who had ventured into the desert without a chaperon.

And the storm hadn't finished with them yet. This was only a lull. What he should do was dispatch her to the spare tent to wait out the weather and then send her on her way with Aban. But he had been a long time alone in the desert and he was only human. The girl was strong and self-assured, mature beyond her years; she knew the score.

He followed her back into the pavilion, noticing how she resented the yards of material flapping round her ankles.

Having forgotten to pick up her skirts, she looked like an ungainly fawn as she struggled to cope with the flowing robe. Big brown eyes and that shock of golden hair peeping out beneath the veil only added to the illusion. He liked her in the veil; it suited her—softened her.

'Is another storm coming?' she asked anxiously, turning to face him as a gust of wind snatched the veil from her head.

'I think we should go back inside,' he advised.

'If there is another storm, how long do you think it will last?'

For a mischievous moment, as he secured the entrance behind them, he was tempted to leave what he was doing and stride outside to sniff the air. But play-acting wasn't his thing. The truth was, he didn't have a clue. They hadn't taught weather forecasting on his course at Harvard Business School.

'What shall we do to pass the time?'

The innocent question was negated by the look in her eyes and his senses, already sharpened by his days of denial in the desert, raged out of control. He found it ironic that the desert had given her to him. The coincidence of them meeting in thousands of square miles of hostile land was incredible, but she had come to him with the dawn—his virgin, Adara. Fortunately, her manner, her eyes, her body language all assured him she was no such thing. When they were both sated and his mind clear again, he would return to Zaddara and take up his duties. This would be his last self-indulgence before duty claimed him.

And now there was only one thing still plucking at his mind. According to Zaddaran tradition there was no such thing as coincidence; there was only destiny.

She went to check her camera and as he looked at her something inside him softened briefly. 'You may take a handful of photographs if you wish—but only of objects and your surroundings. As an aide-memoire for your trip,' he added. He wasn't prepared for the look on her face of sheer surprised delight and found it gave him pleasure to please her.

'That's very good of you. I promise I'll be quick...' She reached for the camera. 'I know I haven't exactly been the easiest guest. Do you forgive me?'

As she turned her face up to him, he wanted to tell her just how much. The appeal in her eyes made his heart turn over which, as far as he could recall, had never happened before. The offer of the photographs had changed something. It was almost as if an understanding, a bond, had developed between them.

She was scrupulously fair and obviously knew what she was doing. She took a few shots of the tent and some objects and then put the camera away. 'There, I've finished. Thank you...'

His gaze was drawn to her lips, reddened where she had chewed on them while she was concentrating on her work. And now there were questions in her eyes: Did he find her attractive? Did he want her? Did he want her enough to make love to her? The answer to all three was, of course, yes. Her lips were slightly parted and damp where she had moistened them. She wasn't afraid to hold his gaze. She was beautiful and she was ready, and she was waiting for him to make the first move.

'Three days and three nights?' She made it sound like a request. And, as she stared at him, his hunger surged to a new level. He had expected many things of his retreat in the desert, but not this forwardness of a young woman who had appeared out of nowhere like a gift…

'And then we will part asking nothing of each other,' he confirmed.

As silence descended between them they both knew it could only have one outcome. And it was a delicious moment that neither one of them wanted to break. It took a ferocious gust of wind to bring her into his arms and, as she rested her head against his chest, he silently praised the storm for wrestling with the tent.

There was barely enough time to inhale Abbas's delicious scent and feel his warmth seeping through the flimsy fabric of her robe before he swung her into his arms. 'We'd ask nothing of each other?' Zara repeated Abbas's words back to him in a whisper.

'Only this,' he murmured, carrying her towards his bed.

She felt so safe that even the sand rattling against the sides of the tent seemed to be in another world. Her body was tuned to his, waiting for his touch, eager to feed on the passion she knew he possessed. He was so restrained, so controlled; to see him lose that was the only thing she wanted now. When he lowered her to the bed she reached up to draw him down to her. Cupping her face in his warm hands, he kissed her deeply. The taste of him was delicious and addictive, the boldness of his tongue the most thrilling thing she had ever known. She wanted more, more of everything, more of Abbas. She wanted every part of him to be touching her and so she clung to him, pressing herself against him until he was forced to hold her away. She made a complaint at once, asking him, 'Why…?'

Abbas smiled against her mouth. 'Your clothes,' he murmured.

Fortunately, she wasn't wearing many, Zara thought, starting to wriggle her way out of the restrictive robe.

'Let me…'

'And yours,' she ordered, impatient to feel him naked against her.

Abbas had no inhibitions and, as he stripped off his robe, she sucked in an excited breath. He exceeded all her expectations. He was the most beautiful man she could have imagined. Resting her hands on his shoulders, she studied him boldly with the eye of an artist. He was like a living statue carved in bronze, with each muscle and sinew clearly delineated. Stroking him, she revelled in his strength and in the way he quivered beneath her touch. The expression in his eyes when he looked at her with approval was intoxicating. He was so big and so powerful and his muscles rippled as they wrestled together playfully. He allowed her to make all the moves, barely touching her, which in turn was the most arousing thing she had ever known. But he knew how to tease and each caress of his hand, each brush of his fingers, lit a separate fire.

Catching hold of her hand, Abbas drew it to his lips. Zara gasped in surprise when he began to suckle each fingertip in turn. She could feel the sensation all over her skin. Crying out for him to be merciful, she sobbed with relief when at last he let her go, but almost at once she wanted him back again. And, when he would not fall in with her wishes immediately, she balled her hands into fists and pounded them against his chest, calling him angry names until he was forced to capture her wrists in one powerful fist and hold them firmly in place on the pillows above her head.

She drew deeply on the fragrance of his skin and sighed with contentment. And, when at last he released her hands, it was her turn to take control—exploring the hard path of muscle, the inflexibility of bone, her fingers travelling slowly and provocatively until it was Abbas's turn to sigh. She enjoyed the sensation of rough chest hair springing against her finger-pads and smiled to feel his nipples harden beneath her touch. Placing both her hands flat on his chest, she drew them slowly down over his torso across the impressive banding of muscle to where she could feel the heat of his erection.

Brushing him lightly, she pulled away when he groaned with pleasure. She hadn't expected him to be so big. The speed and strength of what was happening to her had not prepared her for this reality. And the reality of a man like Abbas was a great deal more than she had expected.

But then he touched her softly, gently, and her courage began to return. If Abbas could tease, then so could she. And she hadn't finished with him yet...

Crouching up on her knees, she used her long hair to brush back and forth across his body, while Abbas made sounds of appreciation deep in his throat. For the first time she knew the power of her femininity and, growing in confidence, she swept her hair across his ribcage, moving gradually lower.

To see Abbas quivering with anticipation was the most intoxicating thing Zara had ever experienced. She found she couldn't stop watching his erection swell and pulse, and as it did so she felt her own body responding to the same urgent rhythm.

And then he turned her so that now she was beneath him. He kissed her again and she whimpered with long subdued hunger. She was feeling everything she had ever hoped for... Abbas's lips, his tongue, his arms, his hands, teasing her and tasting her, enjoying her as she was enjoying him until she could only cry and laugh and beg him to stop before she begged him for more.

Pausing, he raised his head to stare down at her. 'Make yourself clear,' he instructed her huskily. 'Do you want more, or shall I stop?'

'More,' she commanded him, lacing her fingers through his thick black hair, 'I want more...'

Abbas took control then, lifting her to new levels of sensation until every inch of her was trembling and aware. She believed in that moment that it couldn't get any better until he moved down the bed and did something wonderful. Easing her thighs apart with a gentle touch, he dipped his head and tasted her. And then he brought her floating on a river of sensation with his lips and his tongue and his hands. He knew everything he had to do to please her. And, as she gave herself up to him, he slipped her legs over his shoulders to open her more.

Trusting him completely, she closed her eyes. Her world shrank to encompass just the two of them and the sensation steadily building under Abbas's skilful direction. When the storm broke he was ready for her and held her firmly as she cried out wildly as the waves came at her one after the other and with increasing force, until finally, when she had no strength left, they subsided into tiny, delicious little after shocks.

And then she could only manage a single word. 'More…'

Easing her legs off his shoulders and lowering them down gently to the bed, Abbas moved up to her. It was hard to believe that such a powerful man could be so caring, or could possess such finesse and such tenderness.

Zara thought her body must have melted away, leaving nothing behind it but sensation. Everything she had imagined about arousal beneath the hands of a man had been wrong. This was arousal, this stream of sensation through her limbs, the tears of fulfilment streaming down her face, this heightened sense of awareness, the colours sharper, the noises louder, the taste of Abbas lingering on her lips—delicious, spicy, male. And now she could hardly believe how quickly the hunger was returning again. Combing out her hair in strands of gold as she moved beneath him, she tempted him on…

He couldn't wait to possess her. His impatience was that of a boy's, because that was how she made him feel. She had given him so much more than he had anticipated. He had not expected her to be his sexual equal in both appetite and eagerness, but she had matched him and that was not something he had ever expected to find in a woman.

The taste of her, sweet and delicious, still danced on his tongue and the feel of her skin under his hands was the strongest aphrodisiac he had ever known. The scent of her skin and of her hair reminded him of wild flowers billowing in an English meadow and the look in her eyes was bewitching him. When she called out to him he wanted nothing more than to satisfy her need; she had kindled a fire inside him, which he doubted would ever go out. It took all his strength to pause and reach for protection. But he wanted to protect her in every way. And now she was sobbing softly with impatience for him. It made him smile and made him more determined than ever to tease her for a little longer.

Her eyes widened as he drew himself up and touched her very lightly. As he brushed himself back and forth she drew her legs up to urge him on. He needed no urging, but he would not be hurried. He wanted to look at her first, to drink her in, and to see her blush-pink body throbbing with desire for him. Her nipples were extended and tight with need, her lips parted and her eyes black with the same hunger they both felt. She made no false pretence of modesty and when she writhed provocatively he could see every part of her was swollen and throbbing. She was ready for him.

'Abbas,' she murmured, staring at him through half-shut eyes.

It amused him to think he had never needed prompting before. 'Maybe I should make you wait a little longer?' He pretended to think about it, anticipating her complaint.

'I won't wait. I want you now.' Lacing her fingers through his hair, she drew him close.

But still he held himself back and kept her at a distance so that only their tongues could touch, and then just barely. For all his bravado, he wasn't sure that he could wait much longer, and she was intent on making it harder for him with her stroking, searching fingers...

'Do you submit?' she demanded softly.

The wind answered her, moaning languorously, and

then the supporting timbers joined in, creaking in a gentle rhythm that rose and fell like a pulse.

'Kiss me, Abbas… Kiss me now,' she ordered. They were so close now that the smallest movement of her mouth was enough for their lips to brush.

Drawing back, he prepared to take her.

CHAPTER FOUR

HIS senses were tuned to the highest level and so he felt her fear before it even showed on her face. It made him pause. And then he saw everything she was feeling reflected in her eyes—apprehension, tension, dread—and drew back sharply.

'Abbas?' She reached for him, wondering what she'd done wrong.

Rolling away, he sat up and, grabbing his robe, he swung it over his head.

'Abbas, what's wrong?'

'Why didn't you tell me?' Turning, he stared down at her.

'I don't understand...' Her face was flushed and her eyes had filled with tears.

'I think you do.' He stood up.

'Did I do something wrong?'

As she pulled up the sheet to cover her naked breasts, he could see that she had lost the air of innocent abandonment and was already ashamed. Cursing, he stood to secure his robe, and it was then, when he needed interruption the least, that he heard the new sound outside.

'Abbas, where are you going?'

'I have to go out…' There was no time to explain. Raking his hair into some sort of order, he could only rail inwardly at himself. He had misread the signs so badly that he had almost seduced an innocent girl. He had allowed desire to rule him and had closed his mind to the truth. Just the thought of what he had almost done sickened him. And now events had taken over and she would be left floundering because their time together had just run out.

'Abbas, please…'

'Can't you hear? We have visitors.' He turned, impatient to be gone, impatient to cut the ties on a situation that seemed suddenly so squalid and depressing that he couldn't wait to get away.

'Engines?' she guessed, her voice faltering.

'Rotor blades of a helicopter,' he informed her briskly, swallowing his emotions. She was struggling to find her way out of a world of sensuality as well as cope with the sudden change in him, while he had to think of the greater good. There was no time to consider his feelings or hers—he had a country to think of. 'Get up and get dressed.'

As he started for the entrance he caught a glimpse of her sinking back on to the bed, ashen-faced. Pressing her lips together hard so she wouldn't cry, she turned her face into the pillow, but not before he'd seen the expression in her eyes. He felt her bewilderment like a reproach. But, as they wouldn't be seeing each other again, it hardly mattered. They would both have to mark this down to experience and put it behind them.

Zara couldn't believe what had happened and for a good few minutes after Abbas had left the tent she couldn't face it either and kept her face hidden in the pillows. But then she grew furious. Why hadn't Abbas had the guts to face up to her and admit that she didn't please him, that he didn't want her and that she fell short as a woman? His brusque manner proved he had no respect for her. Walking out as he had done had left her burning with shame. She felt ugly and gauche, knowing the closeness they had shared, closeness that had been about to become intimacy. Had it been an illusion of her own making? When he walked out there had been nothing left of the tender lover. It was as if a switch had been turned off and Abbas had woken up and wondered what on earth he was doing with her.

Swinging off the bed, Zara pulled the sheet tight and hurried through the curtain to collect her own clothes. She couldn't wait to wash, to dress, to leave the tent and get away from him. She never wanted to see him again.

So much for her adventure with a Bedouin in the desert, Zara raged silently as she dragged on her clothes. The adventure had drifted away on the heels of the storm—the promised three days and three nights had shrunk to fewer than three hours! And during that time she had played out the role of a naïve tourist providing distraction for a prince of the desert while he waited for the weather to improve and his transport to arrive.

Storming out just as Abbas came back into the tent, she tossed the silk robe at his feet. 'Here, take your robe—'

He didn't reply and only stared at her, his face an enigmatic mask that told her he would not be drawn into an argument. She deduced that whoever his visitors might be, they were still waiting for him outside.

'I'll call Aban,' he said, making no move to pick up the

robe. He'll come for you with the Jeep. You can take some fruit for the journey and some water—'

'Is that it?'

'Should there be more?'

The verbal slap in the face stunned her, but she was careful not to let it show. And then Abbas turned away and walked across the tent as if they were two strangers who had only just met and who owed each other nothing.

Picking up another, more formal, robe, he began to put it on. The *jalabiyya* was long and flowing in regal black and, as he fastened the elaborate belt around his waist, she was stung into reminding him, 'Don't forget your *khanjar*...' Lifting the ornate dagger from the stool beside the bed, she held it out to him. 'No Zaddaran Bedouin is properly dressed without one, isn't that right, Abbas? I believe a weapon of this type is meant to represent your pride and honour?'

Ignoring her cold, accusing stare, he took the dagger from her without comment and secured it in his belt. 'I'll make sure some water bottles are loaded into the Jeep for you—'

'I'm sure Aban will have seen to that—'

She wasn't sure that Abbas had even heard her. He walked away without another word, dipping his head to leave the tent, totally in possession of himself, every bit the tribal leader.

Taking one last look around, Zara found that everything that had so recently enchanted her had lost its appeal. She felt like an intruder, an unwelcome guest who must keep hidden for fear of shaming the host. And yet only minutes before the lion of the desert had been sighing beneath her touch. He hadn't wanted to get rid of her quite so quickly then, she thought angrily, picking up her camera.

She could hear snatches of conversation from outside. The men took it in turn to talk and all of them deferred to Abbas. She could hear relief and respect in the voices of his men and her face burned when she heard their laughter. Was she the subject of discussion? If she was, she damn well deserved it.

'Are you ready?'

Zara's head lifted as Abbas walked back inside the tent.

'Aban is waiting for you.' He gave her a brief head to toe inspection as if to check she looked respectable before showing herself outside.

She ignored it. 'What about my Jeep?'

'My men haven't located it yet, but they will.'

'Please thank them for trying.'

She was all business now, her feelings hidden. At least she'd had years of practice doing that.

She was in Zaddara because she'd had a dream that everything would be clearer to her after the visit, and that she would understand why her parents had loved the country so much they had left her behind in England with her grandparents. That dream was dead now.

Zara clutched her camera tightly as she thought about it. She hoarded images like a miser because her grandparents hadn't been able to face photographs of her parents and had removed every piece of memorabilia from their home. When they had died and she had sorted everything out, she had pounced on a dog-eared album stuck away in the back of a drawer—now that was all she had to remember her parents by.

'It's time to go—'

Zara refocused as Abbas spoke. His voice was harsh as if

he had more important things to do than wait for her. 'I'm ready.' She didn't look at him. She didn't want him imagining the tears that always managed to break through her reserve whenever she thought about her parents were for him.

'Your vehicle will be recovered and returned to you in good condition,' he said as she walked past him.

She calmly thanked him and pushed the entrance cloth aside.

'I will have it serviced… At my expense, of course.'

She stopped and let the cloth drop from her hands as she turned to face him. 'I prefer to meet my own expenses. I took the decision to drive into the desert and the vehicle remains my responsibility.'

'As you wish—' He made an impatient gesture as if to say he had no time to argue the point with her.

In the scorching desert light the military helicopter appeared like a sinister black crow perched on the sand and Zara was surprised to see the squad of men in front of it dressed in army fatigues. A shiver of alarm ran through her as one of them came towards her. She backed away as he raised his gun, but he was too quick for her and tried to rip the camera from her hands.

As she fought him, Abbas saw what was happening and issued a brisk command. The soldier released her immediately.

'I must apologise for the zeal of my men—'

'Zeal?' Zara was furious as she brushed down her sleeve where the soldier had held her. 'Bullies, don't you mean?'

'He was only trying to protect my interest—'

'Save it, Abbas, for someone who might be impressed.' Zara's eyes were blazing as she stared at him.

He glanced at the helicopter. 'This is military equipment and it was your camera they took exception to—'

As Zara cradled it protectively, a hot wave of guilt washed over her. Abbas was right to suspect that she had taken some images that he might not want exposed. It had been a reflex action—he had leaned forward into a shot, by which time her finger was already moving…

'You must give it to me,' he demanded.

'Don't be ridiculous.'

'I don't want to make a fuss.'

'Then don't.'

'I'll need your memory cards too.'

'I can't believe you're saying this. Don't you trust me?' She turned her face up to him and was met by a stare from a man she didn't know.

'The memory cards,' Abbas insisted after a pause, 'and your camera. One of my technicians will go through your images and remove anything I don't wish to be shown—'

His technicians? What business was this man in? 'My answer remains the same.'

'Please.' His voice was clipped; his patience was clearly running out.

She risked one last stand. 'Or?'

'Or I will take them from you.'

She couldn't risk damage to her camera. Grinding her jaw, she handed it over.

'Thank you… It will be returned safely to your hotel when we have finished with it.'

She barely heard him. The camera was her lifeline and now Abbas had taken it from her.

She lifted her chin in time to see him raise his hand to his forehead and dip into the graceful Zaddaran salutation.

'*Ma' a salama*…travel safely, Adara…'

She refused to reply and turned her back when Abbas's helicopter finally lifted off. She would not look up. She would not give Abbas the satisfaction of thinking she cared one way or the other where he went. All she cared about was the safety of her camera.

She should never have come to Zaddara, Zara reflected bitterly walking away to escape the sand flurries drawn up by the rotor blades. She hated the desert. She hated Zaddara. She couldn't imagine what had drawn her parents to such a hostile part of the world, though perhaps it did explain why they had left her behind. Who in their right minds would bring a child to such a terrible place? Most of all she hated him—the man who had told her to call him Abbas. If it hadn't been for the wildlife and some earlier images she had managed to transmit to her computer before he interfered, she wouldn't have had anything to show for her trip.

'What?' Zara turned angrily on the elderly guard, who had chosen that moment to nudge her arm. He was only trying to offer her a bottle of water for the journey, she realised, apologising immediately. 'Thank you…'

As his wrinkled face softened into a smile she felt tears prick behind her eyes. She was teetering on the edge of a full emotional meltdown and his kindness made it even harder to hold on. But that was hardly his fault. '*Shukran*— thank you,' she said again, gently.

'*Ghabel nabud*—it is nothing,' he replied, his eyes glinting with pleasure at her attempt to speak his language.

Before climbing into the Jeep, Zara took a last look around. Images of desert gazelles and the Arabian oryx drinking at the wadi would have to wait now—maybe for ever. The beautiful animals had been a symbol, she realised. More than anything they would have helped her to understand her parents' love for this wild, unforgiving land. But the old Sheikh was dead and she had no friends in Zaddara. There was no one at all who could tell her about her parents.

As Zara watched the arid landscape sliding past the dust-caked window she knew it was time to turn her face to the future. It was that or grow more embittered with each passing year. She had tried walking in the footsteps of her parents and she had failed. Zaddara had been their dream and that was something she would never understand. But back in England she would be free of men like 'Abbas' and his leader, Sheikh Shahin. And she wouldn't let either man ruin her life. She would stage her exhibition. She had enough rage-fuelled energy packed inside her to stage a dozen exhibitions. She could already see the outline in her mind… There would be stark images in black and white of dead creatures, their bones picked clean by vultures… Bleached carcasses against a featureless carpet of sand… Warrior faces turned harsh by aeons of savagery and one face in particular…

The cruel truth of an unforgiving land? Yes, that was her lasting impression of Zaddara and it would make a great title for her exhibition.

CHAPTER FIVE

ANY opening was a nerve-racking event. Would anyone turn up? Would they hate the exhibition? Would they drift around and then move on as soon as was decently possible, wearing tight, embarrassed smiles? 'Will all the canapés dry up before the guests arrive?'

'Will you stop fretting, Zara.'

That wasn't a question, it was an instruction, Zara realised as the older of the two men who ran the city centre gallery admonished her.

'What you've created here is stunning. And if you can't see that…' Lambert paused for a theatrical sigh. 'Then I really don't know what has happened to your eye…'

'My famous eye?'

But Lambert had already floated off in the direction of a lily that wasn't quite standing to attention in one of his fabulous displays and missed Zara's cynical remark.

Lambert was right. She was tied up in knots with nerves. She couldn't relax long enough to look at anything objectively. There was a buzz going round the art world, and all because of this… Walking slowly down the lofty gallery, Zara viewed her images critically. They were shown off to good advantage on the stark white walls. She had opted for colour in the end.

Having started the process of examining the images from Zaddara in an angry, resentful mood thanks to all the bad memories associated with the place, she had been forced to think again. She'd found such an abundance of riches on the returned memory cards and knew instantly that the chance to create something extraordinary was within her reach. Far from a sinister portrayal of a harsh land, she had captured colours and character, shapes and textures, and even a rare glimpse of a sandstorm building beneath a cobalt sky. The flash of humour on an old man's face had surprised her, as had the intricacy of the scroll-work on a silver coffee pot, though that had raised her pulse too. The breathtaking craftsmanship of the goldsmith who had worked on the sheath and pommel of a curving dagger had raised it even more. And, lastly, there had been the silhouette of a man, anonymous and unrecognisable to anyone except her. It was the man who had taken her camera and returned it as promised. The man who had told her that his name was Abbas…

When she had first shown her photographs to Lambert and his partner, Gideon, they had been more excited than she had ever seen them. These were the best images she had ever brought them… She was telling the story of a country in pictures… Zara knew both men were passionate about their gallery and the young artists they encouraged, and for both men to insist that if they didn't have space for her exhibition they would make one…. Well, that had been the moment when she had known she had to put prejudice to one side and get back to work.

And now the exhibition was a sell-out. Which was making her really nervous. She checked her watch again. There were only twenty minutes to go…

At ten minutes before the doors were due to open the exhibition lighting flared on, taking over from the work lights. Colour exploded from the walls and, as she looked around, Zara found it hard to believe it was all her own work. It looked like an exhibition of photographs taken by someone who had loved Zaddara, and she had to admit they took her breath away.

She found her gaze drawn to the far end of the room where the image that had become the emblem of her exhibition took up most of the wall. It showed a Zaddaran Bedouin in stark black relief, with the *howlis* he wore wrapped around his head and face concealing all but a sliver of his autocratic profile. It was enough to make her heart pound. Not black and white after all, but in black, crimson and gold, the colours of the desert, Abbas's image dominated the room. It was the first thing people would see as they entered the gallery.

A ripple ran down Zara's spine as she continued to study the picture. The image held such power and resonance, it was impossible to believe that she had lain in his arms and that for a few hours he had been tender with her. This image showed an elemental force, a man who was at home in the desert and the harsh terrain. Like it or not, Abbas *was* the lion of the desert, he was the fire at the heart of the kingdom of Zaddara.

As a ripple of apprehension travelled across her shoulders, Zara checked her watch again. There were only minutes to go before the doors opened. An anxious glance in the mirror proved she looked as pale as a wraith. She should have remembered lipstick and worn something other than black. Only her hair seemed to have life and colour, but it looked untidy—

'Leave your hair alone,' Gideon instructed, swooping on her. 'Dressed all in black without the suggestion of an adornment, if you screw your hair up in a knot you'll be undistinguishable from a vase.'

'Hush, Gideon,' Lambert observed laconically, peering at her through his pince-nez. 'Zara looks extremely elegant.'

'As she is—with her hair flowing round her shoulders.'

Zara seized the chance to slip away. The first chords of the music she had chosen had just crashed around them and that was the signal for the doors to open.

She could feel the vibrations of the music through her feet and, as the horns pealed out, they tore up the air, shaking the atmosphere with an elemental beat. It was an irresistible rhythm, infectious… Giving in to temptation for just a moment, she closed her eyes and threw back her head to bask in the sound. And now the great doors were opening behind her, but still she didn't move. She could feel the chill damp evening air gushing over her as the art world of London crowded in…

Zara preferred to remain anonymous and mingle with the crowd to pick up whatever feedback she could. But, after being jostled a couple of times, she sought refuge in a corner behind one of Gideon's prized vases, almost knocking it over in her eagerness to escape the crush. Flashing a guilty glance at one of the many security cameras, she remembered that there was no one manning the console. Everyone employed at the gallery was working on the floor in one capacity or another and it was a relief to know her clumsiness would have gone unnoticed. But still she made sure to stay out of the range of the camera. Manned or not, she had the oddest feeling that she was being watched…

'Did you see that girl?'

'I'm afraid not, Majesty.' As far as the Zaddaran ambassador could see, the monitor screen was blank, except for the shadow of a large and rather unprepossessing vase. He had been eager to guide the Sheikh's attention towards other screens showing the images he thought the most appealing, but even they needed adjustment to bring the images into focus and, more crucially, Sheikh Shahin wasn't an easy man to guide.

The ambassador stood back quietly, awaiting his next instruction. The screen hadn't changed, he noticed, though the Sheikh was still studying it.

'No matter.' Straightening to his full height, Shahin waved the ambassador forward, directing him to a seating area where coffee had been laid out for them. 'We'll wait until the crowds have gone and then I'll have a private viewing.'

'I could have the gallery cleared immediately—'

'That won't be necessary…' It was an impetuous visit. *The Desert Unmasked*—an intriguing title for an exhibition. Passing the gallery in the diplomatic car, he'd seen the notice and had asked the driver to slow down. A quick phone call from the Zaddaran ambassador to the gallery's owner and they had been admitted through the owner's own private entrance. That was the way he liked it, low-key and discreet. He never threw his weight around.

'The coffee smells good,' he reassured the ambassador, who clearly felt he should be making things happen, 'and I'd rather wait here.' But his relaxed manner was only a mask for his impatience and he had to ease his shoulders as the enforced inactivity started to get to him. He couldn't view the images properly on the screen; he wanted to get close to them... 'Better still,' he murmured half to himself.

'Yes, Majesty?' The ambassador brightened, sensing an instruction was about to be issued.

'Buy it up... It's easier that way.'

'Buy it up?'

'Yes—everything in the exhibition.' Passing the ambassador a box of small red adhesive dots, Shahin tipped his head towards the door. 'Put one of these on each piece. I want them all, Raschid.' He made a brisk gesture to hurry things along. He wanted to be alone *now*.

This impulsive visit to a gallery was a self-indulgence he didn't have time for. On his return from his retreat in the desert, he had made it a priority to discover the name of his ward. After the incident with the girl Adara he had felt the weight of that particular responsibility more than any other. When his father died it had been a shock to learn that a young woman had passed into his care, but he could understand why his father had assumed the responsibility and he was glad of it. He had felt it too important to send an emissary to reassure his ward that all would continue as before, which was why he was in London. He was here to find her, to introduce himself and to explain...

Easing her way through the crowd, Zara fought her way to the steps in front of the stage from where the image of the

Zaddaran Bedouin stood in silent majesty overlooking the room. The signs were good, but she still wanted to test the mood of her audience. She always needed every bit of re-assurance she could get. A gift she believed had come out of nowhere didn't give you an anchor to hang on to. It hung like a mirage in the air, a fragile talent that might disappear at any moment…

Halfway up the stairs she could see Gideon at one end of the gallery and Lambert at the other, both with their heads tilted at an authoritative angle as they each granted an audience to the art groupies gathered round them.

It really was going better than she had ever dared to hope. But, just as she was starting to relax, she heard a rumble of discontent…

His ward had moved around like a boat without an anchor after leaving school, which accounted for the fact that his people hadn't managed to locate her right away. His father had let things slide towards the end of his life and there had been no record of any last address. To make it even harder, she had channelled every penny she received from the Zaddaran treasury into a number of wildlife charities.

Taking a photograph from his wallet, he studied it again. The stubborn tilt of the chin, the direct stare into the camera…reminded him of someone else. Blanking his mind immediately, he turned his thoughts to what the young woman in the photograph would look like now. She might have changed her hair colour, her name, anything… Pigtails and braces changed to the casual clothes of a young woman about town would make her unrecognisable to the squad of private investigators he had put on the case. Her school should have been able to provide him with a more recent photograph, but it was too late to worry about that now. He could only hope the detective agency had uncovered something he could use. To date they had told him that it was unusual for an individual to have no living relatives, no close friends or partners, *no one*.

The truth had hurt.

'Majesty?' The ambassador hurried back into the room, conscious that his services might be required.

Shahin raised his hand to maintain the silence. He needed a few more moments of contemplation.

Respectfully, the ambassador bowed his head and waited in the shadows.

Whatever the circumstances of the death of his ward's parents, he held himself responsible. He believed himself to be guilty as charged and that was all that mattered, since his opinion was the one he had to live with, Shahin reflected, slipping into a sombre mood.

To say she was disappointed was an understatement. The party had gone completely flat. People were starting to leave and there was a resigned mood as if a promised treat had suddenly been snatched away.

Even some of the most avid collectors were on the move… It made her feel sick inside to think the gallery would soon be empty when they were only half an hour into the night… Desperate for reassurance, she caught up with Gideon and was surprised he could look so elated. She stood to one side, waiting for him to finish speaking to some people as the majority of their invited guests continued sweeping past her towards the exit.

'Gideon… What's happened?' she asked him the moment they were alone.

'Wonderful news,' he said, putting his arm round her shoulders.

'Wonderful? But how can it be wonderful when everyone's leaving?'

Zara was so deflated she couldn't summon up the energy to resist Gideon when, taking her by the arm, he steered her towards a side room where they could talk in private.

Zara waited until he had shut the door. 'Gideon?' She gazed at him anxiously. 'You can tell me the truth now. Don't they like it?'

'What?' He threw his head back with incredulity. 'Everyone loves it, just as I told you they would. In fact, they're ecstatic and I'm not surprised—'

'Gideon, please…' For once Zara was in no mood for the gallery owner's theatrical flourishes. 'Just tell me what's going on.'

'There's to be a private showing, of course, and it's all arranged—'

'You're not making sense. How can there be a private showing when all these people have received invitations for tonight? You can't just throw them out—'

'I hope you don't think I would be so crass.'

Zara shook her head. 'I don't know what to think.'

'Didn't you notice all the "sold" stickers?'

'No…' She'd been too upset to notice anything. Her attention had been focused on the faces of their guests, not on her exhibits.

'Well, here's the good news.' Gideon patted her arm.

'You are a very lucky young lady. A private collector has approached me with an offer to purchase the entire collection—'

'Everything?'

'Lock, stock and barrel,' Gideon confirmed with satisfaction.

'So that was why everyone was so disappointed—'

'I have to admit our guests weren't best pleased when all the red stickers started going up. I'd already had quite a few enquiries by then—'

'Then why didn't you consult me?'

'You forget, I am acting as your agent.'

'I don't mean it as a criticism, Gideon. But to sell everything to one collector… I'm not in this for the money. You know that—'

'Lucky you.' Gideon pursed his lips. 'Not all of us can afford to be so blasé.'

'I'm sorry. It's just a shock for me, that's all.' Zara was still trying to take in what he'd told her. 'I just wish we could have discussed it before everything was agreed.'

'Opportunities like this don't come along every day.'

Zara was forced to concede, 'You're right. You and Lambert have been good enough to host my exhibition and I realise you're not in this business to indulge me.'

'Good girl,' Gideon said approvingly. 'Now, come with me and meet your patron—'

'He's here now? Where?' she asked as Gideon opened the door on the rapidly emptying gallery.

'Upstairs in my office. He wanted this to be a private visit—no fanfares.'

Zara's heart began to race. It had to be someone important, perhaps one of the fabulously wealthy collectors of art who preferred discretion above flaunting their wealth. 'Do I have to meet him?'

'It's usual for the artist to spare a few moments for their benefactor and I think you'll be pleasantly surprised,' Gideon confided. 'I know I was. And if your conscience is bothering you, please don't be concerned about our invited guests because he has requested a champagne reception at the weekend to which everyone is invited. It will be a celebration of your work. Just imagine that…'

This was the pinnacle of her career to date, so why was she feeling so anxious? It wasn't fair to Gideon, or to Lambert, Zara decided. 'I suppose it will be great if we get on…'

'If you don't meet him, you'll never know.'

Tilting her head to one side, she began to smile. 'You're very persuasive.'

'That's my job,' Gideon reminded her. 'Shall we go up?'

Starting up the flight of stairs behind him, Zara nodded her head. 'Are the monitors on?'

Gideon stopped. 'Why do you ask?' One perfectly manicured hand twitched lightly on the banister.

He didn't want any last-minute hitches, Zara guessed. 'I just wondered—if the collector hasn't even been down to the gallery, what made him buy up all the exhibits?'

'A whim? Who can fathom the minds of the super-rich?'

'I suppose…'

'And you know we always do our very best for you. He said he saw the banner outside the gallery. It made him stop the car—'

'Don't you think you should tell me who it is? Prepare me?'

'I've always loved surprises…' Gideon gave her a wink as they reached the door to his private quarters.

How ironic that she should feel so apprehensive at the thought of losing her images of Zaddara when she had almost destroyed them herself, Zara reflected. But now it looked as though she wouldn't be able to keep a single item from her Zaddaran collection. But this wasn't an ego trip and her charities needed the cash just as much as Gideon and Lambert. 'Okay… Let's get this over with.'

'I'd advise you to put a smile on your face first.'

'Will this do?' She pulled a face.

'We're talking tens of thousands of pounds,' Gideon reminded her in an important whisper. 'But if that's the best you can manage, then I suppose it will have to do.'

As all the tiny hairs lifted on the back of her neck, Zara wondered who she was going to find behind the door of Gideon's office. Gideon was quite relaxed, but that was because he considered his part of the job done. He would hand over to Lambert now to put the gloss on everything and provide the smiles and charm that had made their gallery such a honey pot for the *cognoscenti*.

This feeling inside her was ridiculous, Zara told herself firmly. What did she have to worry about when Lambert could charm the birds from the trees and Gideon had a ferociously sharp mind? Gideon would already be thinking about their next exhibition, believing the money for this one as good as in the bank.

Money had never been her main driver, Zara reflected as she walked down the opulent hallway. One day she hoped to find a home for her work that wasn't dependent on sales, but that would take a miracle. For now she had to work as hard as she could for the best result.

Unlike the studied modernity of the gallery, Gideon and Lambert's private eyrie was a testament to their impeccable taste and joint love of all things luxurious. There wasn't a piece of plastic or a chrome lamp in sight, Zara noted dryly as Gideon led the way across the thickly carpeted hallway. Gideon's real pride and joy was the room they were going into next, the room he referred to as his control pod. It had been designed so that he could view all the exhibits in the gallery, though it took his skill to bring them into clear focus on the monitor screens. It was here she would meet the man who had harvested her images as though they were cans of beans in a supermarket sweep. What would he be like? An obsessive collector, she supposed… Older, and possibly reclusive. 'Who is he, Gideon?'

'My client prefers to remain anonymous—'

'Oh, come on, there must be a name on the cheque. Or is he paying you in gold bullion? Gideon?' Zara firmed her voice. 'What aren't you telling me?'

But Gideon had already opened the door. 'May I present Miss Zara Kingston… The artist,' he announced grandly.

She saw Lambert first, standing beside a short tubby man in a dark suit, which reassured her. But then she saw another man standing in the shadows. He turned as she entered, by which time Lambert was advancing with his arms outstretched in welcome.

'His Majesty—'

'I told you, Raschid… No ceremony here.'

She might not have recognised him at once in the immaculate bespoke suit, but the voice was harsh and cold, exactly as she remembered it.

'Gideon, a chair if you please,' Lambert said urgently as Zara swayed towards him.

They connected at exactly the same moment and recognising her had left him reeling too. He drank her in, drank in the familiar upturned face, wanting desperately for time to wind back so he could undo…so many things. It was too much to take in. He didn't want it to be true. The girl he had glimpsed briefly on the monitor screen was Zara Kingston? But Zara Kingston was his ward. *And his ward was Adara—a woman he had never been able to forget…*

His heart was thudding with the shock of recognition, his thoughts and intentions colliding, robbing him of his usual clear thinking. He couldn't conjure up paternal feeling at will towards his long-lost ward, nor could he bring some safe brotherly affection into play. How could he after their encounter in the desert?

He could see that every inch of her was bunched up with tension, and everyone, except Lambert, who had gone to get her a glass of water, was shifting uncomfortably while they waited to see how matters would play out. But she brought it to a head when she turned a look of utter loathing on him, forcing his hand. 'Leave us everyone…if you please.'

The room emptied quickly, the two men gathering up a clearly flustered Lambert as he hurried back in with a glass of water.

'Leave the water,' Shahin instructed, holding out his hand for the glass.

Once the door clicked shut the silence was complete. She didn't move a muscle. Placing the water on a small table within her reach, he went to stand in front of the flickering bank of monitors with his back turned, wanting to give her a chance to get over the shock.

'Can't you face me, Abbas?'

He turned slowly, absorbing the fact that she was a lot more composed than he had expected. Having got to her feet, she held her ground as he walked towards her, but he could see that every inch of her was wound up like a spring.

'Say your name… Say it!' she hissed at him, her eyes burning with hatred.

'My name is Shahin…Shahin of Zaddara.' Relief swept over him as he spoke the words. He felt like a penitent who had finally lashed himself into oblivion. However much she hated him, and she did, for him this was the beginning of his journey to redemption. The tragedy of her parents' death couldn't be shut away any longer and he had wanted to face it for so long.

The air crackled with tension as they stared at each other. It created a powerful energy between them, energy only he could defuse. He had to think on his feet, think how to keep her calm and get her to listen to him. At the same time he had to hide each one of the tumultuous feelings rising up in him, feelings driven by the fact that she was the only woman he wanted, the only woman he knew now that he could never have.

As he lifted his chin he noticed that she was equally determined to remain in control. Proud, strong, determined—those were words that fitted them both. But if strength was their blessing, it was also their curse because, underpinning all that strength, was the shifting sand of the past.

'Shahin of Zaddara…'

She spoke his name softly and thoughtfully as she stared at him, but it was the simmering restraint of impending hysteria and he wanted to avoid that at all costs. She was off-balance, her mind refusing to accept what was happening. Forgetting all his innermost feelings, it was his duty as her guardian to make sure she came round to accepting that she wasn't alone in the world and that, according to the laws of his country, he, Shahin of Zaddara, was legally responsible for her welfare. 'Zara… Can we talk?'

'Talk?' She shuddered as she looked at him as if what had happened between them revolted her now. Hugging herself defensively, she held his gaze with suspicion, as if he only had to move a muscle for her control to break.

'Zara, please—'

'I can't believe I'm in the same room as my parents' murderer. A man who lied to me… A man who couldn't even tell me his real name! Why was that, Shahin? Was it because your name is reviled and because everyone knows what you did? Or was it because you knew who I was and you tried to seduce me deliberately to put a final act to the tragedy?'

'Don't be ridiculous! How could I know who you were?'

'My visa into Zaddara? Your spies? I'm sure you have your ways.'

Her accusation brought him up short. Her visa into the country… When he'd had an army of investigators on the case? Of course, there had been no special warning at the airport and he had been on retreat. The last thing anyone had expected was that she would travel to Zaddara. They had been looking in the wrong place all the time.

'And how do you explain going under a false name?' she continued scathingly.

'Calling myself Abbas was a necessary precaution.'

'I can imagine—' Taking a step back, she raised her head. 'I want to take a good look at you, Shahin. I want to etch every feature, every inch of you, on my mind so I never forget you. I'm going to hold you *this* close for the rest of my life.' As she held her fist to her chest her eyes left him in no doubt as to her feelings.

'You would be very foolish to do that. Why would you allow something that happened in the past to ruin your future? You should be concentrating on building on this wonderful talent of yours—'

'Advice from you, Shahin?' She made a contemptuous sound. 'Excuse me if I don't take it.'

It was hard to argue with her when he was fighting demons of his own. Had their positions been reversed he would have felt much the same. She could only see what was before her and had no access to the truth. 'Stay,' he insisted as she moved towards the door.

'I've seen enough—'

'You must!' He was not used to being thwarted and moved quickly to stop her.

She looked down with furious resentment at his hand on her arm. 'Take your hand off me, Shahin.'

'Where are you going?' He held his hand against the door.

'I'm going home.' She waited with a lot more composure than he might have expected.

He heard the clock ticking the seconds away as he prevented her from leaving. Were the same thoughts going through her mind? She had been prevented from leaving him once before… Holding her here like this did him no credit. He moved away from the door.

The sound of the door slamming rang in his ears as he eased his head back and closed his eyes. Releasing the air from his lungs in one long ragged stream, he faced the fact that this was only a temporary separation. What alternative did he have but to keep her close? Close enough, without ever being able to touch her. Close enough to see the hatred in her eyes every time she looked at him. If she was ever to find the same path to recovery he had she had to know she wasn't alone and that she could always turn to her guardian for support or advice.

Wasn't this the perfect punishment for him? Wasn't this retribution of a type she could only approve? She would be smiling now if she knew the sentence he had just passed on himself.

CHAPTER SIX

THE doorbell distracted her. Dashing tears from her eyes, Zara checked the living room. The room was in a mess and so was she. Gazing at her reflection in the mirror over the mantelpiece, she grimaced. She had two choices: she could pretend to be out or she could fix her face.

Entering the hallway, she slipped into the small bathroom by the front door and ran the cold water. Having dealt with the damage, she patted her face dry and regarded her reflection again. Judging it passable, she straightened herself up and went to answer the door.

Her small modern town house had an excellent security system, which was why she had put a deposit down the moment she received her first decent work-related cheque. The video entry phone was her safeguard at night. She used it now. She sucked in a shocked breath, recognising the face, and then Shahin rang the doorbell again. She could ignore it knowing he wouldn't go away or she could open the door and face him.

'Shahin…'

'Zara… May I come in?'

She left him in no doubt as to her feelings. Standing

back from the door, she made the appropriate gesture for him to enter.

The small hallway led straight into the all-purpose living room. It was living room, dining room and kitchen all in one and she had appreciated the space when she'd bought the house, knowing it to be bigger than the alternatives in her price range. Now it seemed tiny with Shahin standing in the centre of the polished laminate floor. The room seemed to have shrunk around him, drilling home the fact that he was used to spaces on a very different scale.

She didn't ask him to sit down or have a drink, and he didn't patronise her by saying what a nice house she'd got. He was here because he knew he had to tie this matter down and she had let him in because he guessed she never flinched from anything—except once. And he couldn't allow himself to think about that now.

The tension in the small, neat room was palpable. She was mature enough to contain her anger and refuse to let him see how he had affected her, but he wasn't welcome, she made that clear. Without making it obvious, he took a curious look around. He gathered from the lack of personal possessions that she used the house as a hotel, moving endlessly in search of something—an anchor, perhaps. There was only one thing out of place as far as he could tell and that was a litter of photographs spread around the floor. 'You must forgive me for interrupting you…'

'Must I?' Her eyes were hostile.

'I wouldn't have come here, but we must talk—'

'Must? *Again*, Shahin? You seem to forget that I'm not

one of your subjects. I'm a British citizen and I can ask you to leave.'

So why didn't she? He seized the lifeline and pressed on. 'We can't leave things like this. You can't, can you, Zara?' He added an edge to his voice to remind her that the charities she devoted herself to were dependent on the funds from Zaddara.

It proved the tipping point for her. The ice melted and in its place came fire. 'Blackmail now? Why aren't I surprised?' she demanded. 'Whatever you choose to do to me, I won't bend my knee to you, Shahin.'

'That's not what I want. I just want you to understand the past so you can move on.'

'Oh, really? Shahin, the caring citizen? I don't think so. What do you really want, Shahin? What will it take for me to guarantee that money from your treasury keeps on coming?'

She made it sound as if he had gleaned the money from crime, or from the exploitation of those weaker than himself, but he could not allow her to provoke him. 'It's not that simple…'

Her eyes narrowed and he could sense her brain racing as she considered his words and what he wanted. Surprisingly, he guessed she thought none of the possible scenarios entailed her sexual favours. He should have been relieved she thought him indifferent towards her as a woman, but he found himself mildly bemused because she was so beautiful.

'Are you going to tell me what this is about, Shahin? Because if you're not you can leave.' She pointed to the door.

'We need to talk. Neither of us can avoid it, you know that. This has to happen.'

'So you came here to make sure it would?' She looked around as if the house were her sanctuary and he the invader.

'Would you have come to me?'

He had been so careful to keep all the emotion out of his voice and he was surprised to see her eyes fill with tears. Something must have happened before he'd arrived to upset her. As he glanced at the photographs she caught him looking.

'You don't understand anything, do you? You don't understand what you've done because you don't have anything in here...' She clutched her chest. 'You're so busy being a lofty ruler you don't notice the little people on the ground.'

That was so far from the truth it stung him, but he kept quiet, sensing she had to let it out and that there was nothing he could say at this point to console her.

'I saw you looking at the photographs. Would you like to take a proper look?' she cried.

Tears were streaming down her face but she didn't seem aware of them; had she known, he felt sure she would have swallowed them back.

Scooping up a handful, she held them in front of his eyes. 'Take a look, Shahin,' she insisted in a strangled voice. 'This is what you did. You say I must understand the past before I can move on? Well, so must you.'

He couldn't avoid staring at the images...

'That's me at three years old with my grandparents on my birthday...and here's me at four, five and six. Where are my parents, Shahin? Oh, I remember,' she answered for him. 'They were working in Zaddara for you...'

It had been his father, of course, but he didn't correct her.

'Now where's the one of me at seven?' she said in a

much calmer voice as if the storm had passed and her rage was ebbing away. She seemed absorbed in the task of sorting through the photographs.

'Oh, look, here it is,' she said triumphantly, holding it up to him. 'And now it's your turn to tell me what it is…'

Moistening his lips, he gave it a go. 'It's you as a little girl…waiting on a station platform…'

'Yes, that's right. Go on…'

Her voice was calm, and if he hadn't heard the whisper of hysteria just below the surface he might have relaxed. 'You're going on holiday. You're sitting on a suitcase—'

'I was going away to school, Shahin,' she said, cutting him off. 'That was me on my seventh birthday going away to school. I never came home again. You see, my parents were dead by then and I lived with my grandparents. Only they couldn't cope and so your father came up with a solution. Great solution, wasn't it?'

'What do you mean, you didn't come home—surely you had holidays?' But she wasn't listening to him now. She had gone to stand with her back turned to him and was clutching the mantelpiece above the gas log fire. Her knuckles were blue-white with tension. As the enormity of what she'd told him hit him he didn't know what to say. What could he say? What could he do to mend the past? He only knew he couldn't leave her like this.

But as he tried to comfort her she shrugged him off roughly. 'Don't do this to yourself, Zara.'

She made a sound of contempt.

The two sides to his personality battled with each other and the desert won. Dragging her round, he meant to hold her shoulders firmly so she had to look at him, to hear him out—but she landed a double blow on his face before he had time to react. One flat palm and then the next, flying through the air, impelled by desperation and the same longing he felt himself—to once and for all be free of the past.

Capturing her wrists, he held them firmly, bringing her arms down to her sides and holding them there. And when she looked at him with such passion raging in her eyes he did the only thing that felt right—he kissed her fiercely.

She went stiff, as he'd expected, her lips forming a tight barrier she thought he would not cross. But he was stronger and as his will battled with hers she uttered a furious sound deep in her throat. Freeing her wrists, he made the kiss more persuasive. She landed a half-hearted blow with her fists and then another and another, but even as she did that her lips parted and she kissed him back.

But as her fury turned to passion and that passion mounted, his own feelings changed. Repugnance swept over him as he realised what he'd done. He'd kissed his ward in full knowledge of who she was and could find no excuses for his actions this time.

Starting back, he ran his hands down her shaking arms as if that could somehow make everything right again. She was about to say something. He didn't want to hear it.

'Forgive me…' He had to get out.

Zara stood trembling, glad of the mantelpiece to lean against as Shahin strode out of the room. She never felt sorry for herself and the fact that she had broken down in front of Shahin of all people was incomprehensible to her—the fact that he had kissed her and she had let him even more so.

She didn't move a muscle until he slammed the door and only then did she flinch. Her mind was in turmoil. She didn't trust herself to think or move. She was frozen, every part of her locked down.

And then the questions came pouring in. How could she have kissed him? *How?* And how could she have hit him when she abhorred violence of any kind? And then another, more vulnerable voice inside her wanted to know why he had left so abruptly. Did she revolt him?

Zara forced herself to consider the possibility and found it implausible. Shahin had wanted to kiss her. Touching her fingers to her swollen lips, she was forced to accept that she had wanted him to.

And now?

And now her emotions were in absolute turmoil because she couldn't believe she had enjoyed Shahin's kisses quite so much.

The phone rang about an hour later. Zara knew instinctively who it would be. Shahin wouldn't just give up and walk away, conveniently disappear from her life. There was something he had to say to her and, however many doors she slammed in his face, he would find a window and climb through it. And, as her hand hovered over the receiver, unwelcome as it might be, she had to admit to a *frisson* of excitement.

She listened to what Shahin had to say without once interrupting him, but found herself becoming increasingly indignant. He had stirred up a whirlwind and now he was proposing dinner as if nothing had happened. 'No, Shahin—it's too late.'

He ignored the innuendo. 'Supper—half an hour.'

'Shahin, it's almost ten o'clock at night—'

'This can't wait.'

There was command in his tone. He expected her to jump when he gave his orders like everyone else in his world. 'It will have to wait,' Zara said firmly. 'And now, if there isn't anything else…'

'If you want to learn about your parents, you will meet me.'

Every fibre in her body tensed. He had tempted her with the one thing he knew she couldn't resist.

'I'll send my driver to collect you in half an hour,' he said, taking advantage of her silence.

'I haven't agreed to anything—'

'A casual restaurant, no pressure… Busy, impersonal, relaxed.'

Relaxed? Was he crazy? An Arab sheikh in a busy restaurant with all his bodyguards and the protocol that would require…

'Incognito,' Shahin added smoothly, pre-empting her objections. 'We'll wear jeans and enjoy the most discreet protection service you can imagine.'

Go to supper with the man she hated most in the world? He *was* mad.

'Well? Do you want to know what I have to tell you about your parents, or not?'

'You know I do—'

Zara stared at the receiver in her hand as the line went dead. Shahin was a lot harder than the man she had known in the desert. This wasn't her Bedouin Abbas, this was the ruler of a warrior race, Sheikh Shahin of Zaddara, and the Sheikh of Zaddara didn't take no for an answer.

* * *

Zara dressed carefully. Shahin might have said jeans, but she had her pride and that had taken a battering recently. She was wearing slim-fitting jeans with a plain navy-blue sweater and boots. With her hair scraped back into a pony-tail and hardly any make-up, she felt ready for him. No one could accuse her of making too great an effort, but she looked clean and presentable.

As the doorbell rang she grabbed her handbag, not wanting to keep Shahin's chauffeur waiting.

'Shahin…' Zara was stunned as she opened the front door. The very last thing she had expected was that he would come in person to collect her. Instantly she was aware of her bruised lips burning as if he had only just kissed them. 'Were you making sure I turned up?' She knew embarrassment had made her clumsy, but she could think of no other reason why Shahin should come in person to collect her. She regretted the words the moment they left her lips. She didn't want to start the evening on a challenge. She wanted to keep a clear head and make the most of every moment, knowing this might be the only chance she had to find out about her parents.

'I didn't think it right that you should leave the house with a man you didn't know, even if that man was my chauf-feur. I wanted you to feel comfortable right from the start.'

So Shahin had much the same thought in mind. He wanted to keep things cool and polite with everything on an even keel. 'Thank you… That was considerate of you.' She flashed him a thin smile, while her head was still reeling with everything that had taken place between them. Realising she was keeping him hanging on the doorstep, she stood back to let him in. As she closed the door she looked up and down the street, trying to spot his car. It would be oversized and black, with diplomatic plates… 'Did your chauffeur have trouble parking?'

'I gave him the night off.'

'So…'

'We'll be travelling by underground. You don't mind, I hope?'

'The tube?' The station was only on the corner, but she couldn't get her head round Shahin of Zaddara travelling on the underground.

'Unless you'd rather walk?'

'No…no, that's fine.' This was all too casual, too unexpected…

Too clever?

Did Shahin mean to throw her off-balance? He certainly knew how to throw a curving ball, she already knew that. 'I'll just get my jacket—'

She wasn't ready for this, Zara reflected, pulling down her winter jacket from the peg in the hallway. How was she supposed to remain immune to six foot four of solid man who wanted—no, demanded to have a say in her life? A man who could be a prince of the desert one minute and happy to travel on public transport the next. She bitterly regretted losing control in front of him earlier because it didn't exactly put her in a strong position now—neither did seeing him in jeans and a chunky jacket; if he had looked great in a formal suit, in casual clothes he looked sensational.

Shahin was suffering none of her anxiety and appeared to be perfectly relaxed, Zara noticed when she returned to the living room. He was acting as though they were two friends, or work colleagues, meeting up for a casual supper, while her cheeks were blazing and her heart was racing at a ridiculous pace.

'Let me help you with that,' he offered as she started tugging on the jacket over her sweater.

'No, I can manage, thank you. Let's go…' Picking up her keys, she led the way. She didn't want either of them getting the wrong idea about the purpose of the meeting.

The restaurant Shahin had picked was casual, relaxed and about as far removed from the type of place Zara had imagined as it was possible to get. But then she had been surprised by a lot of things about him, not least the way he could change like a chameleon as the situation demanded.

She would do well to remember it, Zara thought as Shahin steered her towards one of the booths where they could expect a degree of privacy.

It would help her to stay calm if she could stop noticing things about him, like how wayward his hair was and how it fell into his eyes until he remembered to push it back. Everyone stared at them as they walked through the restaurant, but she was under no illusion—everyone was staring at Shahin. Not that anyone recognised him; they saw only his power. Shahin gave off a special energy that alerted people to his presence wherever he went.

'This all right for you?' he asked.

'Perfect, thank you…' She sat down, noticing he needed a shave. Although he had probably shaved just before he came out, his hard lean face was already darkened with stubble again. She could imagine the rasp of it against her skin and had to block her mind. She didn't want to be reminded of things that could only distract her, and it was a relief when the waitress came to take their order.

'Would you give us a minute, please?' As Shahin looked at the girl Zara saw her blush.

She couldn't blame the waitress for her reaction. If she hadn't known she was sitting opposite Sheikh Shahin of Zaddara she might have mistaken him for one of his own bodyguards, Zara thought. Like them, Shahin carried an air of danger as well as the power of his blatant sexuality. He was a man of steel, a man of restless energy and, as the young waitress had duly noted, he brought a blaze of glamour to the casual restaurant.

'What's wrong?' His glance flicked up.

A shiver of awareness tracked down Zara's spine as she realised that Shahin always picked up her change of mood in an instant.

'You seem preoccupied?' he prompted.

Preoccupied? Yes! With him! It was so hard to feel angry in surroundings like these—something Shahin had planned, maybe? 'You promised to talk to me about my parents,' Zara reminded him.

'Have you decided what you want to eat yet?'

His voice was like melted honey as he eased back on the padded leather seat, and the waitress was hovering so she couldn't press him now. 'Chicken Caesar and a ginger beer, please…'

'That sounds good to me…' Shahin ordered the same, substituting mineral water for the ginger beer.

They ate eagerly, neither of them having suspected how hungry they were, Zara thought. She certainly hadn't found either the desire or the opportunity to eat during a day that had been packed full of emotion. Glancing up, she wondered whether Shahin had felt the same. Discovering her true identity must have come as a shock to him… His gaze was impenetrable.

When they had both finished eating he surprised her by laying down his knife and fork and starting to talk about Zaddara. It wasn't the subject that surprised her, but the way Shahin began to open up to her. She remained unresponsive to begin with. It wasn't what she wanted to discuss with him. But then she told herself it was a start and that she should find out as much as she could about the country if she was ever going to be able to picture her parents living there.

Against her better judgement Zara found herself drawn in as Shahin started explaining what the kingdom meant to him. Resting his arms on the bleached wood table, he leaned forward in his enthusiasm, his face animated as he laid out his plans.

'But it takes more than talking,' he assured her, 'though we're well into our initial improvements of the infrastructure. Nothing new can be built on any scale until we get that right…'

Zara tried to remain lukewarm; the last thing she wanted was to be ensnared by Shahin's hopes and dreams. But as he talked she realised that everything he wanted was for his people, and she couldn't help but be impressed by the breadth of his vision. It wasn't long before she was prompting him for more information and before she knew it they were exchanging views. She even caught herself smiling in agreement over some of the issues he cared about—education, care of the elderly, better health facilities and improved rights for women. It was only when the coffee arrived that she realised Shahin hadn't broached the one topic they were supposed to be here for.

'Have you changed your mind about pudding?' he suggested when she politely declined as the waitress came forward with her pencil and pad at the ready. 'Another coffee, perhaps?'

'Coffee would be great, thank you. And that was a delicious meal,' Zara added, 'But now we must talk,' she insisted the moment the girl had hurried away.

She felt a tug of concern seeing a glint in Shahin's eyes. Had he planned this all along? Coming out for supper in order to talk had been his suggestion, and now she was pressing him as if she owned the idea. Very clever, Zara reflected tensely, very clever indeed.

Sitting back, Shahin studied her face for a moment and she was forced to hide her feelings. She had to forget tactics and who was doing what to whom and concentrate on making sure Shahin gave her all the information he could about her parents. 'Shahin?' she invited.

'You need to hear what I have to say in context,' he began.

'Yes, I understand that.'

'Do you?' He paused. 'There are certain things you can only understand if you come back with me to Zaddara.'

'Come back with you?' Zara's voice barely made it above a whisper. All she could think was, no wonder Shahin had been so relaxed and at such pains to be an entertaining companion when no doubt he'd known all the time that he was going to drop this bombshell in her lap.

Ice tracked down her spine as she thought about it. A discussion in a local restaurant was one thing—that was in her comfort zone. But leaving England with Shahin to go to a country he ruled, a country where his word was law, was a risk she wasn't prepared to take. 'Surely it won't be necessary for me to come back with you. Things are so easy now—you could email, send photographs—'

'If I believed I could do things that way I would be showing those photographs to you now.'

He let things settle and when he spoke again it was in a voice of reason that was very hard to ignore. 'Once you've made the visit that will be the end of it; you will be able to put the past in context.'

What if it didn't help to explain anything? But would she ever understand what had happened all those years ago if she turned down this opportunity?

She had seen a different side to Shahin in the short time they had been together in the restaurant, Zara reasoned, a human side, and even if she wasn't ready to wipe the slate clean she was impressed that Shahin had proved he shared many of the same goals in life.

'And you should know there's a legacy,' he said, breaking into her thoughts.

'A legacy?' she said in surprise.

'Something of your father's…'

Zara's eyes widened, but then she frowned. 'If it's money, I couldn't possibly take it. You'll have to find a suitable charity…' Any thought of profiting from money her parents had earned for a job that had led to their deaths was unthinkable.

'It isn't money,' Shahin assured her. 'I think you will find it a lot more valuable than that.'

Zara looked at Shahin, wanting to believe him.

'So you'll come back with me?'

A legacy from her parents worth more than money hung between them like a sparkling chalice. Shahin knew she would be unable to resist it, Zara reasoned. He also knew that she was uninterested in material possessions. She hadn't used any of the money from Zaddara for herself, and her home was simple. So the legacy must amount to an emotional journey into the past, which was all that she had ever wanted. But she wasn't prepared to take everything Shahin said at face value and decided to probe a little deeper. 'If my father had left a legacy I'm quite sure I would have heard of it by now…'

'Can you take that chance?'

Zara bit her lip, not wanting him to see how much his offer had tempted her. Shahin might be lord of all he surveyed in Zaddara, but she would exert her will when it came to her father's legacy; she would not have him controlling it. 'Whatever this legacy is, I want it to stay in Zaddara. My parents loved your country, that much I do know. Perhaps I could raise a small monument, something modest. I think they'd like that…'

Her voice had changed and grown small… She had been so sure and confident up to that point, but now her expression was bleak. The truth was, she didn't remember her parents well enough to know what they would have liked and that shamed him. He owed her parents a debt of honour. She had to come back with him so she could understand—not why things had gone wrong, but how much they had achieved. And he wanted her to understand why her mother had decided to leave her in England. But there was another reason, Shahin admitted to himself, and that was he couldn't bring himself to let her go.

'If you come to Zaddara you'll know your parents as well as I do.' He meant well, but as he saw her eyes widen with resentment he knew that all his persuasion had been for nothing, thanks to that one fatal error. She couldn't bear the thought that he, Shahin of Zaddara, the man she held responsible for her parents' death, might know them better than she did.

And then a bad situation turned rapidly worse.

With a mumbled, 'I'm sorry... I shouldn't have come here—' she pushed up from the table, dropping her bag in her haste and scattering the contents across the floor.

As he dipped to help her, she scrambled to hide some photographs from him.

'Don't,' she said furiously, snatching them out of his hand.

'But I've seen the others...'

'And so you don't need to see these.'

It looked as if she kept them with her always, he thought as she stuffed them without looking into the side pocket of her bag. But what she didn't know was that he still had a couple in his hand.

His bodyguards, having spotted the disturbance, had started moving out of the shadows and at the same time a young man from a neighbouring table looked as though he might interfere.

'Call your men off, Shahin!' Zara demanded.

As she leaned across the table to make her point, he found his gaze drawn to her breasts. Some demon inside him demanded to know why he hadn't enjoyed them when he'd had the chance—and then guilt rained down on him.

How could such thoughts be possible when he had accepted the fact that she was his ward? 'Sit down, Zara—' He spoke sharply but discreetly so that only she could hear, knowing there was no time to lose if they were to avoid an unpleasant scene. His bodyguards were within arm's length of the young man. 'Everything will return to normal if you do,' he assured her. 'Turn around. Smile at your young champion. Let him know you're all right. Reassure him, Zara… Now.'

After the briefest pause, she did as he asked and as he saw the man settle back in his seat and the bodyguards melt away he sat down too.

He put the photographs he hadn't given her yet face up on the table between them. 'We shouldn't have any secrets. We have to be honest with each other.'

'I don't want your sympathy,' she said, putting her hand out to take them back.

Quick as a whip, he covered her hand with his own. 'No. I want to see them.'

Her mouth worked. He could tell that the last thing she wanted was another opportunity for him to see her with her guard down. 'No sympathy,' he promised rashly. 'Curiosity, that's all.' He held her stare until she relented.

Picking them up, he realised at once that she must have kept them all, some would say obsessively. It explained a lot about her feeling for the camera he had confiscated in Zaddara. While it had been in his keeping he had felt her anxiety curled around it like a living force and had been glad to get rid of it. He had been more than relieved when she had emailed him to confirm its safe return.

There was one photograph for each year she had been

at school. They all showed a pale, defiant child, her mouth fixed in a rictus grin, surrounded by happy warm-hearted people. They were family photographs—only one of the children was a cuckoo in the nest and it didn't take much insight on his part to know which one. He could see that all the families had gone out of their way to make a child who had nowhere to go for the holidays feel at home. And on each of the photographs she was with a different family. He understood everything now and his heart ached for her.

He was careful to keep every suggestion of emotion out of his eyes as he laid the photographs down again. Leaning forward to look her in the eyes, he insisted, 'Come back with me, Zara. Come back with me to Zaddara…'

CHAPTER SEVEN

THE Ruby Fort...

Zara hadn't known what to expect when Shahin told her on the flight over that this was where they must go if she was to claim her father's legacy.

He hadn't warned her that they would be travelling to the fort on horseback, something he might have rethought had he known she would be sharing his horse. And any thrill of clinging on to Shahin had been more than wiped out by a level of discomfort she could never have imagined in her wildest dreams...

They had been riding for the best part of an hour and every bit of her was saddle-sore. She hadn't known how much longer she could go on. But as Shahin's favourite palace rose out of the empty desert like a mirage she soon forgot about her aching body.

As they drew closer Zara could see ramparts taking shape. Sunset was the time when the palace was at its best, Shahin had said, and he wanted her to see it for the first time just like this...

He was right—it took her breath away.

The colours in the desert were always stunning, but

tonight they were exceptional. The sun hovered on the horizon like a big orange ball, glorious and effulgent, as if to remind the world of its splendour before plunging the land into night. Every colour was exaggerated—the mountains blacker, the sand turning rapidly from ivory to copper, while the sky was a mesmerising mix of lavender and tangerine. And still against this artist's palette of colours the Ruby Fort stood out.

The name alone sounded like something out of a fairy tale and the Ruby Fort did more than live up its reputation. As the name suggested, it blazed red thanks to the countless gems implanted in its walls—gems that had been a gift, Shahin had told her, to his father from the tribesmen who had wanted to show their gratitude to the elderly Sheikh who had laid his wealth at their feet.

'What do you think?' he said, turning his stallion side on to give her a better view.

Before she could answer, he cried, 'Get up, Jal!' and Zara's cry of alarm was lost in a flurry of hooves as Shahin pointed his horse towards their destination. Zara barely managed to lodge her thighs around the stallion's side in time to prevent herself bouncing off. She had been foolhardy enough to try and ease her aching leg muscles by lifting herself a little way out of the saddle and had almost paid for it with a tumble.

'Enjoying the ride?' Shahin asked when he finally reined in.

Gritting her teeth, Zara ground out, 'Great'. How could anyone enjoy riding? Zara wondered. And, as for finding it comfortable… Shahin might be able to sit deep in the saddle, completely at ease, but she felt as if she might possibly be damaged for life.

'Good,' he approved, urging the stallion forward again. 'I told you you'd soon get the hang of it…'

As the horse surged forward Zara clamped her teeth together to stop them rattling in her jaw. She felt like a sack of potatoes and her only wish now was to make it to the fort alive. And the first part of their journey had gone so well—a limousine, a private jet, a royal car waiting for them on the tarmac… Their luggage, Shahin had explained, would be taken on ahead by helicopter. And so she had suspected nothing when the chauffeur-driven royal car had drawn in to his riding stables. She had relaxed by then, fearing helicopters more than anything—except for horses. The green tinge on her face must have given this away and the horse they brought out for her had been swiftly re-stabled.

Resigning herself to the ride, she could see the Ruby Fort was growing even more impressive as they drew closer. When Shahin slowed their mount to a trot beneath the battlements it gave her a chance to appreciate the scale of the palace as well as the care with which it was maintained. As they clattered over the ancient drawbridge Zara's neck was aching from gazing up the towering walls to stare at the crenellated battlements where pennants were flying in honour of Shahin's arrival.

Zara gasped as they rode on through the great gates and entered a courtyard vast enough to house a small village. A mass of white-robed people were waiting there to greet their leader and the moment they saw Shahin they roared their approval, raising their arms in a tide of welcome.

Holding on round his waist, Zara could feel Shahin's

voice vibrating against her hands as he called back to them. Self-consciously, she quickly released her grip.

'Well?' he said, turning to her. 'First impression?'

'Fantastic… I'm overwhelmed,' she said honestly.

Zara was relieved when the stallion slowed to a walk, but her cheeks heated up again when Shahin took him at a deliberately slow pace through the ranks of people. She was provoking considerable interest and knew his people had to be wondering why their leader had a dishevelled woman clinging to his back. Putting a hand to her hair, she quickly straightened it and fixed a composed expression to her face. Then, sitting straight, she tried to look as if riding came naturally to her and she wasn't aching in every part that had contact with the horse. But the truth of it was she was in agony and she couldn't believe anyone was fooled.

Shahin reined in at the foot of the sweeping marble steps. There was a clash of arms as he dismounted and rows of men clad in the graceful robes of Zaddara dipped into a deep bow as he returned their greeting.

Zara realised that she hadn't fully appreciated Shahin's position up to that moment. In the traditional robes he had changed into before leaving the aircraft he was both awe-inspiring and magnificent. She watched with interest as a manservant advanced respectfully. He was carrying a beaten copper tray upon which she could see two tumblers and a jug full of some refreshing drink. Ice clinked enticingly as the man walked closer—and suddenly she couldn't think of anything else but how thirsty she was. Grabbing the horse's mane, she tugged her right leg over its back and started to dismount. Distracted by one of his men, Shahin didn't see what she was doing…

Zara was proud of the neat way in which she was dismounting—until she reached the ground and discovered that neither leg would support her weight.

'Curtseys are unnecessary,' Shahin assured her dryly as she exclaimed with shock. And then, turning to the line of dignitaries, he added, 'May I present Zara Kingston.'

Trying to raise a smile for them and a scowl at Shahin wasn't easy, particularly when she was sprawled in a heap on the ground. This wasn't quite the entrance she had planned. And when Shahin offered to help her up she was forced to admit, 'I don't think I can walk—'

'In that case…'

Zara gasped as Shahin swung her into his arms. Moving swiftly down the line of carefully impassive men, he took her up the steps and in through the grand entrance of his desert home.

'This is your room… I hope you like it?'

Like it? Zara had to cling to the ornately carved back of a sofa when Shahin lowered her to the floor. She still didn't trust her legs to function properly. It was hard to take in everything at once. It was more ballroom than bedroom and the truth was that she felt lost in the vast room.

A sumptuous gilded bed dressed with satin sheets and a crimson quilt was raised on a central platform. There were steps up to the bed and she could only imagine what would happen if she woke up in the night and missed her footing. Several open archways led off to what she supposed must be other rooms, robbing the bedroom of any cosiness it might have had, and hovering in the background a number of serving women were waiting for their instructions. 'This is too much!' she exclaimed softly.

'Don't you like it?'

'It's magnificent, Shahin, but—'

'But?' he demanded.

'Well, don't you have anything smaller?'

'Like a cupboard?'

'No, like a bedroom where I'll feel cosy and where I won't be staring at the shadows and wondering if they're moving half the night.'

He had put her in this suite of rooms for a very good reason. The suite was as far away from his own quarters as it was possible to get in the palace. He wanted her out of his way, out of temptation's reach, and if by settling her into the Presidential Suite was what it took to accomplish that—

'Really, Shahin, I'm not happy about this.'

He had to hide his astonishment that anyone would turn down the opportunity to experience such magnificence. But as she turned her face up, waiting for his response, he suspected she wouldn't be easily persuaded. It forced him to race through the possible alternatives in his mind. It wasn't as if the Ruby Fort was short of rooms, but all the guest rooms were on a similar scale. The smaller family rooms were all situated on his side of the palace.

'It would only be for a couple of nights. You're not planning to stay any longer, are you?' He hoped that would be an end of it.

'I won't be staying overnight if I have to sleep here.'

He should have known she was as stubborn as he was.

'All right, I'll see what I can do. But, in the meantime, why don't you take a bath? I'm sure you'll find the bathroom to your liking.'

'You mean I smell of horse?'

She could imagine what she liked—he had new preparations to make.

'So I do smell of horse. Will someone show me where the bathroom is, please?'

A woman advanced immediately, bowing to him as she drew close.

'Don't worry about finding your way around the palace,' he told Zara. 'I'll have them bring you to me when you're ready.'

On a golden litter? Zara wondered, holding Shahin's gaze. Even then the pictures in her head couldn't compete with the murals on the walls. She wouldn't have been surprised to learn that he had housed her in the harem. 'Shahin—' Her voice stopped him at the door.

'Yes?' He turned to face her.

'Will you show me my father's legacy tonight?'

'Later, Zara… At dinner… We'll talk about it then.'

But she wanted to know about it now, Zara thought, watching Shahin's shadow disappearing through the archway. He had brought her here on the promise that she would be told everything, and now she had to wait again?

'I'm sorry,' she said, remembering the woman waiting to look after her.

'Please let me know if I can get you anything else,' the woman said in perfect English after showing her the bathroom. 'There is a bell here…and here…and here…'

Zara wasn't used to being waited on and felt uncomfort-

able. 'Thank you, I can manage… You've been very kind.'
It was as polite a dismissal as she could think of.

'Shall I have your cases unpacked while you bathe?' the
serving-woman asked her.

'Well, I'm hoping to move to another room, actually—'

'Just one outfit for dinner, perhaps?'

'Thank you… Cream silk pants, and there's a topaz-
coloured blouse on the top of my other clothes…'

The woman bowed and then beckoned to her compan-
ions. 'I will return in one hour and take you to the Sheikh,'
she said respectfully.

That sounded ominous, Zara thought, and one hour
didn't leave a lot of preparation time. In fact, it was far too
short when every inch of her was aching after jiggling up
and down on the back of Shahin's stallion. That thought
only grew when she walked into the sumptuous bathroom
and discovered that it was the size of her living room at
home. Clad in night-dark rose-veined marble and lit with
scented candles, it was equipped with every luxury product
she could imagine. There were fluffy rugs underfoot and
a hot tub bubbling gently in one corner with fragrant petals
strewn across the frothy water…

She would just have to put her concerns on hold while
she soaked her aching limbs, Zara decided, throwing off
her clothes.

Bathing in such fabulous surroundings was too good to rush
and Zara left it to the last moment to climb out of the hot
tub. She had to dress quickly to be ready when the serving
woman arrived to guide her through the palace. As she
hurried all her feelings of apprehension came rushing back.

Why hadn't Shahin told her about her father's legacy? She liked to know facts right away so she could deal with them, and she would have preferred to deal with them on her own ground, not Shahin's. Whatever her father's legacy turned out to be, she wanted the opportunity to view it in private. It was too much emotion to share with anyone, especially Shahin. Though, in fairness, everything that had happened since meeting Shahin in the desert had challenged her beliefs regarding him. She had created a monster in her mind, but when she had met the man she had found him too complex to be easily condemned. His magnetism alone made her feel as if she was betraying her parents, but it was hard to know how she should ignore the feelings he provoked. And particularly here at the Ruby Fort she was finding it impossible to forget what had happened between them the last time they had been in the desert...

A discreet tap told Zara the time for thinking was over. She had always known this would be difficult, she told herself firmly. She just had to get on with it, face Shahin and find out what he could tell her about her parents and their legacy.

The marble floors seemed to go on for ever and as Zara walked behind the serving-woman she had plenty of time to regret her decision to return to Zaddara with Shahin. She should have held out in London and insisted he tell her everything there...

Gazing up at the towering golden doors, Zara had to wait until two men in flowing white robes belted in crimson silk opened them for her. They bowed low as she entered and as the serving-woman slipped away Zara couldn't help thinking that she had been well and truly delivered to the Sheikh.

Shahin rose as she entered. Dressed in flowing black silk robes, he looked magnificent. Zara stood for a moment taking everything in. The brilliant room was a perfect frame for his darkly dramatic looks. There were ivory columns decorated with gold leaf stretching up to a stained glass cupola above his head, and the rich jewel shades of the glass were reflected in velvet cushions and plush deep-cushioned couches set around the room. A feast had been laid out for them on a low table and in an alcove musicians were playing softly. The air was lightly scented with sandalwood and candlelight flickered on gold filigree sconces…

It was only then she realised she had left her camera in the room. She subdued the urge to rush back and get it. Polite interest was the most she could afford to show if she didn't want Shahin thinking she was so startled and overawed by her surroundings she couldn't hold a proper discussion with him.

'I thought we'd eat here, seated on cushions in the Zaddaran way…'

He indicated a place where she might sit across from him on a mound of silken cushions. As Zara moved deeper into the room she was conscious of her pulse racing.

'I hope you approve?'

A low table laden with delicious delicacies would divide them. On closer inspection Zara decided it might have been polished bronze or even gold. Whichever, it was quite a contrast from the wine bar she would have gone to at home! She tried to tuck her legs neatly beneath her as Shahin was doing so effortlessly. But her limbs hadn't recovered from stretching over a ton of horse and refused to cooperate so she ended up sitting to one side, trying to look as if she found this comfortable.

She was about to speak when an army of servants, responding to some invisible signal, began to serve them and each time their plates were cleared away another course followed until she found herself becoming edgy. She was deeply conscious of the minutes ticking away and wondered if Shahin intended getting down to the discussion as he had promised. She would have to start the ball rolling, Zara decided, when he finally waved the servants away.

'That was delicious, thank you. And now—'

'Your father's legacy?' Shahin anticipated. 'It's something you need to see, rather than to talk about, Zara.'

Zara bit back her disappointment. She had come this far and her goal was so very close, but she had to be mature and tell herself that after waiting so long she could be patient for one more day. 'I'll see you in the morning, then,' she said, trying to get up.

'I thought we could talk a little first about your exhibition…'

In fairness, Shahin had bought her entire collection of pictures and this was a good opportunity for him to flesh out his understanding of her work, Zara reasoned, sinking down again. 'What would you like to know?'

'What drew you to photography?'

The harmless question allowed her to relax and Zara found herself telling him everything, from the school magazine to the present day. She couldn't help noticing that the excitement she always felt when she talked about her work had not infected Shahin and wondered why he was looking so concerned for her.

'You seem to do so much of this alone,' he commented with a frown.

'All of it.' Zara looked at him quizzically, wondering if Shahin thought everyone had a team of experts to call on as he did.

'Doesn't working alone get to you?'

'No, why should it?'

She was absolutely sincere, Shahin realised, and he could tell that she didn't have a clue what he was getting at. He pushed a little more. 'And when you come home, don't you have friends to come home to?'

She wrinkled her brow. 'Of course I have friends, Shahin. I kept the friends I made at school—wonderful people. But we all lead busy lives. We don't live in each other's pockets, if that's what you mean.'

'So you never feel lonely?'

'I don't have time to feel lonely,' she assured him. 'How can I, when I'm so lucky with my work?' She leaned towards him. 'Shahin, I'm surprised at you. You live a very similar life to me—a solitary life, and you're not complaining…'

The similarities between them had never struck him before, but he realised now, to his surprise, that she was right. People had surrounded him since the moment of his birth, but they were all paid to attend him. Was there anyone he could confide in now that his father was dead? Anyone he could trust enough to be completely relaxed in their company? The answer to that was, of course, no.

The realisation that his ward was not a victim as he'd thought her, someone to be swept up and sheltered, but an independent woman who saw herself in a very different light to the way he did took some getting used to.

'Shahin?' she prompted, anticipating that he would agree with her.

His answer was to press a discreetly positioned call button with his foot.

Had she gone too far? Zara wondered when Shahin didn't answer her right away. She guessed it was the first time anyone had risked comparing their mundane sort of life to his. But even when she ran over it again she could only draw the same conclusion. Was she supposed to suck up to him and humbly agree that of course her life couldn't possibly be compared to that of the ruling Sheikh of Zaddara? She wouldn't take a word of it back. The fact was she loved her life and had thought Shahin was pretty pleased with his… And they did have to work alone for much of the time—that was just the way it was.

Zara tried to get the conversation going again, thinking it time Shahin shared some of his experiences with her. This was supposed to be a two-way conversation and not a trial where she was the only witness. But he appeared to be distracted and, following his gaze, she saw that the serving-woman had returned and was hovering by the entrance.

'A smaller room has been found for you,' Shahin said, standing up. 'I hope it meets your requirements. Fariah will show you where to go.' He dipped into the traditional bow, prompting Zara to get up.

'What about our conversation?' she reminded him.

'It can wait until tomorrow—when we're both feeling rested.'

And, before she could protest that she was wide awake,

he added, 'We leave at dawn. Dress for the desert… Something comfortable with shoes you can walk in.'

Zara's cheeks flamed red as Shahin turned away. The Sheikh had dismissed her, she realised angrily, and there wasn't a thing she could do about it.

CHAPTER EIGHT

THE following morning Zara had too much pent-up excitement inside her to worry about Shahin's curt dismissal the previous evening, or the fact that he appeared to be determined to keep his distance now as they walked together down the palace steps. Having been told to dress for the desert, she was wearing cool cotton trousers with a loose-fitting long-sleeved shirt and desert boots, while Shahin was wearing jeans rather than his long flowing robes. In the past when he had worn jeans she had found it to be a sign that he was relaxed. Eastern dress seemed appropriate for the reigning sheikh—casual dress was Shahin without the trimmings. She hoped this was one of those more relaxed times and that he would open up to her, but his aloofness warned her she might be setting her expectations too high.

A Jeep stood waiting for them in the courtyard and a male servant was standing beside the driver's door holding the keys. Thanking him in Zaddaran, Shahin told her to get in.

Zara stopped dead and looked at him. This journey into the desert to learn about her parents was everything she had dreamed about, but she could not tolerate Shahin's behaviour towards her. She had done nothing wrong. She would rather Shahin gave her directions and left her to find her father's legacy on her own than suffer his brusque manner. 'Not until you tell me where you're taking me—'

'Get in and I'll tell you—'

'Open the door for me and then I'll get in.'

She could tell her defiance still had the power to astonish him. Apparently no one ever argued with the Sheikh of Zaddara. Maybe a good argument was what he needed, Zara reflected—it might help to unbutton him… Maybe it would do them both some good! She felt as if she might burst from holding in all the things she wanted to ask him. She closed her eyes tightly as she fought for control. And then was surprised to hear determined footsteps striding round to the passenger side of the vehicle. It was an even bigger surprise to see Shahin wave the servant away and open the door for her himself.

'Hurry up,' he said brusquely.

Progress? Zara wondered.

They headed out into the desert and after about an hour or so of driving Zara thought she had never known Shahin so tense. 'Is it far now?'

'This is just the start of your journey.'

Zara decided to skip the innuendo and stick with the facts. 'That's a bit vague for me—how about a destination?' She had to grip the handle on the side of the door to stop herself from falling on top of him when Shahin brought the Jeep to a skidding halt.

'Do you want to know about your parents, or not?' he snapped, holding her angry stare.

'Of course I do—'

'Then understand that this is hard for me too.'

'Hard for you?' All the resentment she had pushed aside came pouring back.

'Yes! Show them some respect!' he said passionately.

His level of concern for two people she thought exclusively her own came as a total shock to Zara and she didn't take it well. 'You dare to lecture me about my parents?'

'If you can't see I'm trying to help—'

'It's a little late for you to help me, don't you think?' Grief, loss, frustration—everything welled up in her at once. 'You were responsible for the death of my parents and, not content with that, you went on to seduce their daughter—'

'And you were so unwilling?' Shahin cut across her. There was only so much he could take and she was testing all his limits.

Zara's face blazed with passion but she held her tongue and gradually the tension inside the confined space fell back again.

'Shahin, I'm sorry,' she said at last. 'You're right. I'm just as responsible for my actions as you are. It takes two to…'

He started the engine. This was hard for both of them—just how hard for him she would never know; he had really cared about her parents, and still felt terrible when he thought about the tragic waste of life.

'We're going deep into the desert,' he explained. 'The place doesn't have a name. But I can get a satellite fix if you would like to see its whereabouts on the monitor screen…'

'Thank you, I'd like that,' she said after a moment, adding, 'What kind of place is it?'

'The first oil exploration site we had here in Zaddara. It's a place you need to see if you're ever going to understand what your parents had to put up with, what brought them here and why they stayed... And, most important of all, why they left you behind.'

He felt her emotion without looking at her and as he drove he tuned in the satellite navigation system so she could see the site on the screen. 'Here,' he said, drawing her attention to it.

'Thanks,' she said as he made some necessary adjustments to the screen.

In his peripheral vision he could see her studying what he'd shown her. He wanted to show her the first camp and explain what the broken-down buildings represented. It wasn't something he could delegate, though admittedly it would throw them together at a very vulnerable time for her. Some base part of him wanted to tell her the truth and have it over with. At one time Zara's father had been considered the finest geologist of his generation but, having turned to drink, he had become reckless and unpredictable. His father, Sheikh Abdullah, had taken a chance on hiring him, mainly because he couldn't afford anyone else. Luckily the calculated risk had paid off for Zaddara, but not for Zara's father or for her mother...

He had always thought Zara's mother a gentle lady with a spine of steel. It was she who had held it all together until the moment her husband, full of drink, had decided not to wait, but to use the faulty detonators after all.

The circumstances didn't matter now, Shahin reflected, ramming his foot down on the accelerator. He held himself responsible for the death of Zara's parents and would always do so. In his naïvety he had believed he could buy detonators cheaper on the black market. His father had picked up the flaw in them immediately and had ordered him back to Zaddara to replace them with quality products from a reputable supplier. He had been nineteen at the time and trying to play his part in rescuing an impoverished country, and in doing so had caused the tragedy. He had rushed from the desert to Zaddara and back again in a single day to replace the equipment but had been too late. It was a miracle his father had survived. But he had killed Zara's parents as surely as if he had fired the faulty detonator himself. Whatever anyone else thought, he would never forgive himself for that.

'Would you like me to take over the driving for a bit?'

His ward's question made him leave the past and drew a smile to his lips. 'I think I can handle it…'

His smile deepened at her murmured exclamation and he had to wonder what he had to do to stop wanting her… If it hadn't been right before, when he hadn't known who she was, it was even less so now. But nothing, not even the fact that she was his ward, seemed to make the slightest impression on him.

Swinging the wheel, Shahin pointed the Jeep towards the deepest and most hostile part of the desert. It had taken great courage for her parents and his father to explore this particular region in the early days before any form of infrastructure had been put in place and he wanted Zara to know that. He had to concentrate on getting there and forget how many things he wanted to do with her, to share with her, and that they beat at his brain every waking moment. Each time he was with her like this, within touching distance, was only ever going to remind him that she was out of his reach.

* * *

It was just a collection of ramshackle buildings. They had been driving deeper and deeper into the desert and all the time she had been straining to catch her first sight of… Well, that was just it, Zara realised—she hadn't really had a clear idea of what to expect, but this wasn't it.

She felt shivery as she climbed down from the Jeep and then foolish as tears pricked her eyes. But nothing could have prepared her for treading the same land, seeing the same horizon, staring at the same sky that her parents had. Talking, asking questions… None of that filled in the gaps like this collection of time-scarred trailers. But, instead of providing answers, the exploration site only provoked more questions… How could her parents have existed here? How could they have left their small child for this? She didn't understand and she wanted to so badly, yet now she was here there didn't seem any hope she would find any of the answers to her questions.

The site was just so desolate, Zara thought, hugging herself as she looked around. Then she noticed Shahin staring at her and remembered he had been driving for hours… She couldn't let him see how disappointed she was.

Seeing her looking at him, he came around the Jeep and put his arm across her shoulders to urge her forward. 'This building was where your parents lived…'

Shahin's brief, comforting squeeze worried her and she braced herself for what might come next. She turned as always to her camera. 'Do you mind?' she said, lifting it. 'I'd like to make a record…'

'Of course,' he said, standing back as she ran off a series of shots.

However unpromising the trailer looked, she wanted

him to know she was all right. And she did want a record of everything so that perhaps in time she could understand. Having finished, she headed off towards the door. But when she reached it she hesitated, waiting for Shahin. It took her a moment to gather her resolve.

He opened the door for her and then stood back.

Zara's first impression, aside from the overwhelming heat as she stepped inside, was disappointment. Disappointment and frustration… There was just a table, three plastic chairs and a stiff broom that somebody had left leaning against the wall. The sight of the broom gave her a pang… It was as if the person who had left it would be back any time now, but the lack of personal touches, of personal possessions, made her feel as if she had been robbed.

Judging the moment right, Shahin walked across the room and opened another door. Without needing to be asked, he sensed her need to be alone and didn't attempt to follow her as she went to explore.

It was a bedroom… An iron bed was pushed up against the wall and through another smaller opening she could see a basic bathroom. Remembering her own opulent quarters back at the Ruby Fort, Zara grimaced. 'Is this it?' she whispered.

'No, this is just the beginning,' Shahin assured her. 'I thought you should see how it was for them when they first set up camp. The place grew, of course, as the work progressed…'

She looked out of one of the windows when Shahin pointed and saw more buildings.

'This was the first portable building on site,' he explained.

'Thank you for showing it to me… '

'You know how they had to live now—how hard it was for them.'

What wasn't he telling her? Zara wondered. 'And?'

'How tedious it was for them back then when they had finished work for the day… No satellite phones, no TVs, no outside communication of any kind, unless they had visitors… And I'm guessing even playing cards and reading palled after a while.'

Zara was sure Shahin was hiding something and if there had been problems caused by stress and isolation she wanted to hear about them. 'But my parents had each other,' she pointed out, 'and then there was your father…'

Shahin refused to respond to her prompt. 'I hope this tour will help you get everything in perspective,' he said economically as he made for the door.

Zara followed him. 'I knew it was going to be basic…' She still hoped to prompt him into revealing why he had suddenly withdrawn into himself.

'It's more than a lack of amenities that makes life in the desert so hard,' Shahin explained. 'It's the emptiness, the space…' He stood by the open door, looking beyond them to where the horizon was smudged by a heat haze. 'It's gets very lonely out here…'

'But there are more buildings,' Zara pointed out. 'Weren't there more people?'

'We couldn't afford any more people, but the buildings sprang up as the work continued. There was a lot of equipment and that needed storage space.'

'Can we go and see those buildings now?'

'Of course…'

The largest of the buildings had been used as a makeshift

recreation hall, Shahin explained. It was here that Zara would find quite a few things belonging to her parents…

She prepared herself mentally, but when Shahin hesitated outside the door she found her confidence draining away. 'What's the problem?' she pressed.

'Nothing…' Shahin looked deep into her eyes. 'I thought you might want to look around here on your own, that's all…'

'Good idea…' She forced a light note into her voice.

He released the catch without opening the door fully. 'I'll be waiting for you in the Jeep.'

He got halfway to the Jeep and then turned back. He couldn't leave her. Whatever demons he might be fighting, someone had to be there for her—he had to be there for her.

He was feeling everything a guardian should feel, Shahin told himself, walking faster. She'd been on her own for five minutes—five minutes too long.

Treading carefully, he made it to the door and stilled his breathing to listen. Racking sobs, almost completely smothered… He guessed she had her head buried in her arms; she never wanted anyone to know how she felt. He didn't hesitate. Maybe it was an intrusion, but it was something he had to do. He found her sitting in the centre of the floor, leaning against the leg of the dusty pool table and, surrounding her like a moat of memories, were the photographs he knew she would find. 'Zara…'

'Leave me… Please, Shahin. I want to be alone.'

'I thought you should know where your own talent comes from…' She didn't ask him to leave so he pressed on. 'Your father was a brilliant photographer, as you can see…' When his hand wasn't shaking too badly to hold a camera, Shahin remembered grimly, keeping that thought to himself. 'He kept a record of everything that happened on site from day one—'

'Just as I would have done…' She forced a smile as she looked at him and then gathered the photographs in. 'These are wonderful…'

As she picked up a handful of photographs to study them, he knew the time had come to tell her everything. 'Searching for oil saved my father at a time when he was out of his mind with grief at the loss of my mother in a smallpox epidemic…'

'Oh, Shahin, I had no idea…'

The way she so quickly forgot her own concerns touched him deeply and he knew he could hold nothing back from her. 'It was particularly ironic that since the day he took the throne my father had fought to raise the standards of health care in Zaddara. But there was never enough money. He believed oil was the answer and that was when he brought your parents on board. He couldn't offer them much, but they shared the same vision…'

'So the continuing health risks explain why I was left behind in England when they came to work here?'

'Exactly,' Shahin confirmed, feeling they had drawn closer than they had ever been in that moment.

'Go on,' she pressed.

'This was their headquarters—no air-conditioning, no heating… Freezing cold at night and dangerously hot during the day. My father used to sleep on that old camp bed over in the corner, while your parents used the mobile home you've already seen. They lived in primitive conditions, but there was no money to spare. It was an all or nothing venture for them.'

'So I share the same thirst for adventure…'

'Yes, I think you do,' he agreed.

'And what were they like?' she asked eagerly. 'Can you tell me? Do you remember?'

He thought how best to phrase it before saying, 'Of course I do. Your father was a brilliant man, fiery and impetuous… Your mother far less so. She was his rock.' She'd had to be strong, Shahin remembered, she'd had a lot to put up with. 'But as far as diplomacy went?' He was longing to make it easier for her. He wanted Zara to understand where she came from, but he wanted to leave her with happy memories of her parents; they had done so much for his country. 'Your mother always said exactly what was on her mind,' he confided, hoping to lighten the mood.

'You're saying diplomacy wasn't her strong point?'

'Does that remind you of anyone?'

She almost smiled. 'How did she behave towards your father?'

'As if being the ruler of a country was no big deal.'

And now she did smile, but she looked away.

'Shahin,' she said at last, 'I think it's time you told me about the accident…' Her voice was low and quite steady, but she wasn't quite ready to look at him.

He was determined now to take the line that would hurt her the least. 'You know about the faulty detonators.'

'And you knew too,' she said softly.

'We all knew they were faulty,' he admitted. 'My father had detected the fault and had insisted they be locked away until they could be safely destroyed. He sent me back to Zaddara to buy more.'

'So, what went wrong?'

'I wasn't here, but…'

'My grandparents were quite clear that it was your fault.'

'I'm not trying to mislead you. I take full responsibility.' He refused to make excuses for himself. 'I bought the faulty batch cheaply from a man who worked in army ordinance. I thought I'd done a good deal. I never dreamed there'd be anything wrong with them.'

'You were young—'

'I was nineteen. But, young as I was, I would never have knowingly risked lives to save money.'

'So what did happen?'

He phrased it carefully. 'Your father was eager to get on with things…' Then he paused.

'Do you mean he took a chance and broke into the place where the detonators were being kept? Shahin,' she pressed when he hesitated.

He wasn't comfortable with telling her that this was exactly what had happened. 'He was close to finding oil…'

She frowned. 'And you didn't get back in time to prevent him from using the faulty detonators?'

'I shouldn't have bought them in the first place.' Emotion made his voice harsh.

Zara paused for a second, considering what she had heard. 'However long it took you to get back after concluding the new deal, my father had no right to break the locks, nor was there any excuse for him using detonators he knew to be dangerous.'

He could say nothing, because her father had been

drunk. He had been blown clear by the explosion and had died later in hospital, while her mother had perished in the fire. His father, Sheikh Abdullah, had been lucky. He had been standing where they were now, taking delivery of some more equipment. He wouldn't tell her everything, Shahin decided. There was nothing to be gained by telling her the truth about her father and breaking her heart all over again. 'We all made mistakes that day,' he said simply.

'And you still blame yourself for taking so long to get back here? It's a long drive to Zaddara, Shahin.'

'I know that…' He ground his jaw; he didn't want her making excuses for him, but still she had a right to know. 'I drove to the capital and back in less than twenty-four hours. In that time I sourced the new detonators, had them checked and arranged payment.'

'You did all you could—'

'I hold myself responsible to this day,' he said, cutting across her. 'I know money was short and we were so close to finding oil we could almost smell it, but I was offered a deal and at the time it seemed the only way we could push things forward. I sold the Jeep to pay for the new detonators when I arrived in Zaddara and then I rented it back from the man I sold it to, to make the return journey. That's how hard up we were—'

'But oil was found?'

'Yes, in one final irony, the explosion that killed your parents uncovered oil. But, as we both know, it was discovered at far too high a price and, whatever you or the world thinks of me, I will never forgive myself.'

She sat in silence on the floor, surrounded by her

photographs, until at last she whispered his name and looked up at him.

'Yes?'

'I want to thank you for your honesty… I know you believe you were to blame, but you were all adults, and all responsible for your actions. You were only nineteen, trying to do the best you could for your financially crippled country. And if my father had only waited for your return the accident need never have happened…'

He was determined to protect her. 'Don't feel you have to absolve me.'

'But I must,' she insisted, 'because you will never forgive yourself until I do. The accident was my father's fault, Shahin. His eagerness killed him, not you. And you mustn't blame yourself any longer.'

He needed no more absolution than those words. And he was glad for Zara's sake that she had been able to accept his account of her father's part in the tragedy. What good would it have done to tell her that her father had been drunk and that alcohol had prompted him to take the fatal risk? It would taint her memory of him, and that was all. 'Thank you,' he said with more feeling than she knew. And then, because he couldn't leave her sitting on the floor a moment longer, he drew her to her feet.

Emotion grabbed him when he saw she was still holding some of the photographs to her chest. 'They've been waiting for you—' He had to turn away.

'Yes, and now I understand who I am,' she told him simply, 'thanks to you, Shahin.'

As she spoke she touched one of the photographs and there was such an expression of longing in her eyes that, without thinking, he drew her close. He could feel her trembling as he stroked her hair and as she pressed into him it was as if she needed to feed on his strength. He stroked her back, willing her to relax, until with a ragged sigh she turned her face up to him.

She was waiting for him to kiss her, he realised. Their faces were just inches apart. He tried to force himself not to look at her lips—lips that were softly parted and moistly inviting... But taboo. He settled for a quick hug, releasing her while he still had the will to do so. And when she wasn't quite quick enough to hide her bewilderment, he thought quickly and said, 'Come on... There's something else I want to show you—'

'What is it?'

She looked so worried. And who could blame her when the sexual chemistry between them was snapping like an overloaded power line?

Slipping his hands into the pockets of his jeans before he could be tempted to take her hand, he said, 'Wait and see... I think you're going to like it—'

As Zara stood with Shahin outside the largest of the buildings she wondered what secrets it held... And why was Shahin edging away from her? It didn't make sense. After stripping away years of hurt and anger in the past hour he couldn't think she still blamed him for the accident. She felt a profound sense of loss as she walked around the site, but the only anger left in her was for the people who had supplied the faulty detonators.

'This was going to be an exhibition hall—'

She looked up as Shahin began speaking again.

'It was something they always joked about,' he went on. 'They used to say all they had to exhibit were blisters on their hands, but that one day it would be different... They were far-sighted people, Zara, your parents and my father. They could see past their difficulties to a future when Zaddara would be prosperous and they knew that the next generation would want to know what their country's wealth had been founded on.'

She could never hear enough about the past, and even more so now, Zara realised, because it was a heritage she shared with Shahin.

'I want to use those photographs you found back there,' he explained. 'I want to exhibit them—with your permission, of course. In fact, why don't you help me with the project? You've got the know-how and perhaps we could involve Gideon and Lambert?'

'They'd like that...' She hadn't expected Shahin to push things along at such a pace. Now she understood why the kingdom of Zaddara was rising like a phoenix out of the desert since Shahin had taken control.

'We'll have the pictures,' he went on, 'and then we'll bring all the artefacts out of storage and create a museum—'

'Shahin, that's a wonderful idea...' It was impossible not to be swept away by his enthusiasm, but as she rested her hand on his arm to show her appreciation he moved away. He was in the middle of sharing his vision with her, Zara reasoned, and let it go.

'I can see your images of Zaddara here, can't you?' He turned to look at her.

'Yes, I can,' she admitted. It was everything she had ever dreamed of...and what both sets of parents would have wanted. As emotion swept over her she tried to hug Shahin and was shocked by the brusque way he shook her off.

Zara couldn't believe she had misread the situation so badly. She was stunned by the fact that Shahin found her gesture of affection so distasteful.

'Where are you going?' He stepped in front of her as she tried to leave.

'I'd like to go back to the Jeep—'

'But I haven't finished showing you round yet—'

'I've finished looking.' The expression in her eyes left him in no doubt that she was serious.

'There's something I have to tell you…'

'Something else?' Her mouth tightened. She couldn't think of anything so important that Shahin had to stand in front of her like this.

Pulling a document out of his back pocket, he handed it to her. The royal crest of Zaddara was prominently displayed on the thick cream vellum.

'What is it?'

'Why don't you read it?'

Filled with curiosity, Zara turned away from Shahin. After a few moments she wheeled back again, laughing in disbelief.

'Why are you laughing?' Shahin demanded quietly.

'Because this is absolutely ridiculous… Because I have no intention of holding to an agreement like this—' She thrust the document towards him.

'It's a legal document,' he said, refusing to take it. 'It's not up for discussion.'

'Legal here in Zaddara, maybe…'

'I think it's better if you keep it, don't you?' he said calmly when she tried again to hand it to him. 'For your records…'

'I don't want it.' She tried to give it to him again and, when he refused, exclaimed, 'If you won't have it, it can go in the bin.' She looked around and, finding no bin to put it in, she screwed it into a ball and flung it down on the floor at her side.

'Destroying the document means nothing,' Shahin told her calmly. 'The facts contained within it hold firm.'

'Facts?' she exclaimed in outrage. 'The only fact is that that is the most preposterous piece of patronising cant I've ever read.'

'I'll leave you to think about it for a moment, shall I?'

'I don't need a moment,' Zara assured him, turning away. Her cheeks were on fire. She couldn't remember ever feeling quite so worked up. Sheikh Abdullah had been her guardian and now Shahin had inherited that role? What was worse, according to Zaddaran law, Shahin would remain her guardian until she reached the age of twenty-five.

She wouldn't accept it. It was that simple.

CHAPTER NINE

'How old are you, Zara?'

Shahin addressed the question to Zara's hostile back. His tone was so reasonable it only made her angrier. 'You know how old I am. My date of birth must be written on your precious document—'

'How old?' he asked her again in the same level voice.

Shahin must have known she wouldn't accept this, Zara raged internally. Did she need a guardian? *Did she?* And then the penny dropped… This was why Shahin had been so distant with her since he'd kissed her. This was why he was avoiding physical contact with her like the plague. He could attribute a moment's loss of control to any number of things, but more than that was unthinkable as far as Shahin was concerned. But why couldn't he have been straight with her from the start? 'I'm twenty,' she told him fiercely, still stinging from his distant manner, 'As I'm sure you know—'

He ignored her fury and continued in the same reasonable voice. 'So we have five years to make this work.'

'Five years? Don't tell me you intend going through with this?'

Shahin's silence assured her that he had every intention of doing just that.

'But I never had any personal contact with your father. So why should we change things now? The money from Zaddara has always been paid on time without my ever meeting Sheikh Abdullah—'

One ebony brow rose. 'That sounds like a very mercenary arrangement to me… I fully intend to take an interest in my ward's life, as I hope she will in mine—'

'She? This is me, Shahin,' Zara reminded him furiously. 'And don't you dare make it sound as if all I care about is money. You know as soon as I could support myself I channelled every penny of the Zaddaran funds into my charities.'

'But the money was paid—' he flashed back softly.

Anger was getting her nowhere, Zara realised. Taking a deep, steadying breath she tried to reason with him. 'I can't believe you'd want to enforce this agreement, or that you'd expect me to go along with it.'

'I'm not above the law, whatever you might like to think, and if I flaunt this official order, or allow you to do so, what does that say to my people?'

'But this is wrong. Can't you see that?'

'Not in Zaddara; here it is the law.'

'Then the law will have to be changed.'

'That's not as easy as you think, and even if it could be changed it wouldn't be a quick fix. What we have is a binding contract between us. I don't want to argue with you—'

'Then let me out of this agreement, Shahin,' she said, cutting across him. 'I'm my own woman, responsible for myself. You know that…' Ward and guardian was one relationship between them Zara knew was never going to work.

Shahin's expression darkened. 'I thought my bringing you here had set things straight between us.'

'Don't, Shahin,' Zara warned. 'Bringing me here isn't a blanket solution for everything…' Even as she made the complaint and did everything in her power to push him away, her heart yearned for him. She hadn't suspected the depth of her feelings for Shahin until this moment, Zara realised, and the irony wasn't lost on her. Shahin was further out of her reach now than when the great chasm of her parents' death had stood between them.

'What about our museum?'

She faced him calmly, knowing that if she stayed on in Zaddara and helped Shahin to create a showpiece museum their relationship would be platonic—that was what he was telling her. But the project they both cared so much about would be completed. It was agony to balance a long held dream against another, no less intense for the fact that it had so recently come into her life. But in the end, Zara accepted, she could only do what was right. 'A museum that would stand as a monument to our parents…' The slight inflection in her voice turned it into a question.

'Of course…'

Shahin kept his expression neutral as he waited to see what Zara would say. She had suffered two surprises, two traumas, in quick succession. He had been wrong to be surprised by the intensity of her reaction. And now he had to wait and see if she had as much character as he thought. To stay true to his original intention he must remember that his intention had been to find his ward to explain that he would be taking over her guardianship, and to reassure her that everything would remain the same…

His jaw clenched at that. *How could it remain the same?* It must, he ordered his inner voice. 'You would have separate accommodation, of course,' he informed her. 'And, naturally, you would have a voice in all the decision-making.'

'A voice?'

He had to hide his feelings at the small victory, but adrenalin was pumping through his veins at the thought that she might stay. She had to stay. He needed her input, her expertise… 'An equal voice to mine,' he amended, moving away from the door. The project would be nothing without Zara's fire, her creativity, her vision… For that alone he would put up with her challenging him every inch of the way. It was worth it to build something so special and unique. But now he wanted her answer. 'Will you stay? Yes or no?'

The look she gave him left him in no doubt that it wouldn't be an easy ride for him. And then she spelled out the specifics.

'To create a museum that would celebrate my parents' achievements and those of your father? Yes, I'll stay for that.'

A second rush, bigger than the first, ripped through him. Duty would make this work. It had always kept him focused in the past. He had vowed to serve his country and they would be so busy once the project kicked off that neither of them would have the opportunity to think about personal considerations. Transforming the old building into a world-class gallery would take every moment of their time… But it would take a day or two to get everything in place, a day or two during which both of them must be kept fully occupied. And then he hit upon a solution…

'Where are you going?' she called after him as he headed off.

It pleased him to think she was calling him back and he didn't stop or slow his pace.

She ran faster than he had ever imagined she could on the sand and was there, staring him in the face, by the time he reached for her door handle. He hid his surprise and didn't waste time talking. 'Get in…' He left her to clamber in and shut the door for herself.

She flared a look at him as he sprang in beside her and surreptitiously clung on as he slammed the door and gunned the engine.

'Where are we going? I think you'd better tell me. Or is this another of your surprises, Shahin?'

He was taking her to a place where she could relax, making it easier for him to persuade her to accept the contract between them.

'You could say that…' He swung the wheel.

'So,' she prompted doggedly, 'where are you taking me?'

He ground his jaw, knowing this wouldn't stop until she got everything out of him. 'To my desert encampment—' To counter her stunned silence he added, 'Not the camp site where we first met—this is a different place… I hope you like it.'

'I hope I do too.'

Her voice augured trouble if she didn't! But it pleased him to keep the surprise to himself for now. He wasn't taking her to a spartan Bedouin tent but to his favourite place of recreation—a desert encampment where he was able to indulge himself far away from prying eyes and where Zara would see the obvious benefit of being his ward.

Just as he expected, when they crested the hill she exclaimed in amazement. He pressed her for a reaction.

'It's hard to imagine all this is here after…'

As her voice tailed away he guessed she was thinking about the desolation of the oil exploration site where their parents had lived and worked. But they had all worked for an outcome like this…this was Zara's heritage as much as his and she had every right to share it with him.

After a pause she asked him why the exploration site had been allowed to get into such a state.

'In his later years my father couldn't bring himself to go there. It upset him too much…'

'I'm sorry. I should have realised…'

'But restoring it is at the top of my agenda,' he reassured her.

And mine, her eyes seemed to tell him.

'So… What do you think?' Drawing the Jeep to a halt on the hill, he leaned his elbows on the steering wheel to stare out over the luxurious encampment.

'It's amazing…'

Her enthusiasm gave him a warm glow of pleasure. He was so keen to help her look to the future.

'It's not what I expected at all,' she went on. 'It looks so…'

'What?' he prompted, his lips tugging up in a grin, 'Fabulous? Regal?' She was right to be surprised—no one knew of this place except his most trusted advisors.

'Are you teasing me?'

He was so pleased by her lightened mood that he laughed, enjoying her surprise. He couldn't wait to get down to the camp and start spoiling her.

In the soft evening light the canopied pavilions were pale shadows against a lilac-coloured sky. The sand had deepened to mustard-yellow and the naked torches added exclamation marks of flaming crimson to the peaceful scene. The colours alone were spectacular, but just for once Zara had forgotten to raise her camera, Shahin noticed. Dusk was a very special time in the desert, but it looked as if she would have to come again to take her photographs...

The rush of pleasure that thought gave him augured badly for reining in his feelings where his ward was concerned. He realised he was already planning her next visit to this very private and sybaritic retreat.

The pavilions were clustered around the most beautiful stretch of sapphire water Zara had ever seen. 'Oh, look...' Her heart thundered with excitement to see birds skimming the surface of the oasis. There were men flying falcons, she realised, and beyond them camels standing in a palm-shaded paddock. And then she saw the horses and her smile died abruptly.

'You're going to learn to ride,' Shahin confirmed, as if this was the greatest gift he could bestow on her.

'Oh...wonderful.'

'And you're going to have the very best instructor there is.'

'You?'

He frowned. 'Of course me...'

As Zara's heart picked up speed she didn't want to think if apprehension or excitement was the cause of it. But maybe learning to ride wouldn't be such a bad thing after all...

Was this her tent? No. How could this be called a tent? Zara wondered, turning full circle beneath the vaulted ceiling.

The pavilion into which she had just been shown was absolutely stunning. It was impossible not to feel pampered the moment she walked beneath the canopied entrance.

Shahin had been right to say she would find this a very different experience to his Bedouin tent. Gazing around, she guessed the furniture and all the beautiful ornaments must be antique and suspected that many of them were priceless treasures. The room was scented with exotic aromatics and candles flickered in what she was sure were solid gold holders. The bed was of a type she had never seen before except in a magazine. Huge and circular, it was dressed with crimson satin covers beneath a mirrored canopy.

As she crossed the room to explore the rest of her accommodation, she trailed her fingertips over sumptuous fabrics and jewelled *objets d'art,* hardly able to believe that all these riches had been brought into the furthest reaches of the desert to satisfy one man's desires. It showed another and far more intriguing side to the serious-minded Sheikh of Zaddara…

As her heart drummed a warning, Zara forced her attention back to her surroundings. Better not to think about Shahin in any light other than His Royal Aloofness—unless she wanted another knock back during her stay.

If she had thought the bedroom of her suite fantastic, the bathroom exceeded all Zara's expectations. Cloaked in ivory pink-veined marble, there was a hot tub big enough for two and a walk-in shower. Through another doorway she discovered decking, beyond which her own private swimming pool glinted in the fast fading light. The wrap-around veranda overlooked the oasis, which was softly lit by torchlight now. Then she noticed that a table had been laid for her, complete with fresh fruit punch sitting on a bed of ice and delicious-looking canapés.

'Do you like it?'

At the sound of Shahin's voice every part of Zara's body tingled. He was standing directly behind her and when she turned she saw that he had already changed out of his jeans and was wearing a flowing robe. The scent of his cologne teased her senses and because his ebony hair was still a little damp she knew he must have used the time to take a quick shower. 'I like it very much…' In the muted light his robe, beaded discreetly black on black around a deeply slashed neck, showed off his tanned, toned body in a way that stole her breath away.

'Good,' he said, hopefully missing out on the fact that she was somewhat distracted.

She had to try very hard not to react when he came to stand by her side.

'This is where we will indulge ourselves before getting down to work,' Shahin explained.

'Indulge ourselves?'

'In vigorous exercise,' he said as if that were obvious. 'That way we can free our minds for the work that lies ahead of us.'

Very commendable, Zara thought wryly.

'Why are you smiling?'

Because the thought of vigorous exercise with Shahin had a certain appeal. And because she'd plucked out three words from what he'd said, Zara thought mischievously, and given them a meaning all of her own… Indulge. Exercise. Vigorous. 'Perfect,' she said aloud. 'I mean, it's perfect here,' she said when he looked at her with suspicion. And then, widening her eyes, she added earnestly, 'And I'm sure a vigorous workout will give us both the best possible start.'

'Good. In that case we will start your riding lessons tomorrow at dawn.'

'At dawn?' Zara bit her lip. She wasn't sure she wanted to wait so long.

'The horses have been fed,' Shahin explained to her, smiling at her eagerness. 'They need to rest now. But don't worry,' he added, thinking no doubt to console her, 'we'll be ready to ride out at dawn, before the sun makes things too uncomfortable…'

If there was one thing she had learned from fending for herself it was that she couldn't sit around waiting for things to happen—she had to make them happen, Zara reflected. 'Couldn't we start my lessons tonight?'

'Ride in the moonlight, do you mean?' Shahin frowned.

Zara held her breath.

'You're not sufficiently experienced to take the risk— riding at night can be tricky'

'Then how shall I ever become experienced if you do not teach me?'

Raising his head to the stars, Shahin cursed softly in Zaddaran.

So he had got the point. 'Shahin?' Zara felt a thrill of anticipation as she pressed him. She wasn't letting him off the hook now.

But just when she was confident he'd got the message, his face changed. 'What are you trying to do to me, Zara?'

Firming her jaw, she stared him out.

'Don't you know who I am?' His voice was low and rough and he gripped her arms in his passion.

'If I ever forget I'm sure I can rely on you to remind me, your royal highness—'

'Forget my title! I'm your guardian! You're my ward! How do you expect me to overlook that fact?'

'I think you'll find there's plenty of historical precedent for—'

'For what?' He cut her off brusquely. 'You're still a child—'

'I'm twenty years old,' Zara argued fiercely. 'I'm a woman, Shahin, even if you can't see it. I'm old enough to know what I want—'

She was right. And she was everything a woman should be and never had been. They had all been too eager, too obvious, too desperate, but Zara fought him every inch of the way. There was nothing desperate about her—other than her desperation to have her own way and defy him at every turn. But he loved the fire, the fight he could see in her eyes. 'And you know what you want?' he mocked, unable to resist the temptation to provoke her.

'Yes I do!'

'And what's that?'

'You…'

They glared at each other for a moment as if hate and not passion had fuelled the exchange. The air was charged and alive with danger and Shahin knew he was battling an enemy he had no hope of defeating, because that enemy was himself.

He kissed her brutally, hard, as if the guilt was pouring out of him and she had to absorb it and make it right. But, whatever it said about Shahin's feelings for her, he could not possess more determination than she did to have him make love to her. She was all sensation, caught up in passion, need, love, desire… This was her man and she had laid claim to him.

Was it wrong for a guardian to love his ward? Who said it was wrong? Who had the authority to pass judgement? Could a man-made law stand between lovers? Who dared to deny fate?

Zara thought her heart might burst with happiness when Shahin swung her into his arms.

Now she was lying on the bed he kissed her gently and stroked her hair, but she cried out in disappointment. She was ready for him. She had been waiting so long she didn't want to wait a moment longer. He knew she wanted fast relief, but he knew better. Her lips might be plump, her nipples thrusting towards him through the fine fabric of her shirt, but he would refuse her what she craved. He would tame her a little first and show her the benefits of patience.

Capturing Zara's wrists in one fist, Shahin brought them over her head and rested them on the soft bank of pillows.

'Don't stare at me as if I might break,' she complained.

His lips curved with amusement. 'Don't touch, hold back, or you might break… Is that what you think I'm doing?' he teased her in a low voice.

'Shahin!' she warned him furiously as he dropped kisses everywhere on her face except her mouth. Her frantic need for sex was arousing him more than he had ever known.

'You're looking at me as if I'm one of your delicate ornaments…'

'Would you rather I was rough with you?'

'Yes…'

'Well, you're going to be disappointed.' He had to ignore the angry sound she made deep in her throat and concentrate on keeping her still.

The pain she had read about would all be over in a moment, Zara reasoned. What was Shahin waiting for? Did he think she couldn't stand it? She would bear anything to have him claim her, as she had claimed him. She wanted all of him and she wanted him now, every part of him. At first, as she writhed beneath him, she thought he was holding her still so he could lecture her on the error of her ways—perhaps lay out another, more prosaic, exercise schedule for the next day… But when Shahin dipped his head and ran the tip of his tongue across the full swell of her bottom lip with tantalising steadiness she realised that this was all part of the foreplay and her senses roared to a higher level still.

Her lips were so sensitive after his earlier rampage she cried out in excitement, and then groaned with sudden pleasure as he rasped the stubble on his cheeks against her neck. She arced her body to find contact, but he cleverly moved away, denying her the touch of his hands and the possessive thrust of his tongue until she was going mad for him. Could anything be more arousing? She writhed shamelessly, hunting for relief, even from the friction of her thighs and from the pleasant sensation of her hips moving on the cool white sheets. But Shahin refused to be hurried and her actions only deepened the half-smile on his lips.

'And that was your first lesson, little one,' he told her, apparently unmoved by her sharp growl of complaint.

'To wait?' She challenged him angrily. But he only gave

her impatience a moment's hearing before teasing her with his tongue again. A sigh of delight poured out of her as Shahin began to toy with her ear lobe, and he soon had her angling her head, wanting more. When he pulled away she moved sinuously beneath him... And, with her hands still trapped in his fist, she stretched out her body to lure him on— arching, sighing, trying everything she knew to make him forget his wretched rules on control. Which got her nowhere.

When at last he let her go it was to start unbuttoning her shirt, which he did with a tantalising lack of urgency. She thrust her breasts at him, eager to show them off and have him approve them. She couldn't wait to see the look on his face when she was naked and he could dip his head to suckle. But as she lifted her shoulders from the bed to speed things up, he pressed her down again. And all the time Shahin's eyes were burning into her, assuring her that he knew how much she wanted him and that the more she urged him to hurry, the longer he was determined to make her wait.

CHAPTER TEN

'WHY are you holding back like this, Shahin?' Zara challenged him impatiently.

'Holding back?' His voice was husky. 'There are certain benefits to delay, as you will discover when you are more experienced…'

'Are you patronising me?'

'Would I?'

She ignored the obvious and went for the subject closest to her heart. 'And shall I grow more experienced beneath your hands?' She felt a sense of power seeing a muscle jump in his jaw. 'How much do you want me, Shahin?'

His answer was to take her mouth with mind-numbing thoroughness while he chafed her nipples beneath the flimsy lace of her bra.

Lifting his head, he teased her cruelly. 'Let me think…'

As she cried out Zara knew that her bra had proved no defence against Shahin's determined assault, and that both her lips and nipples were swollen with arousal by the time he had released her.

Slipping his hands behind her back, he freed the catch on her bra and cast it aside… And then the real torture began. Her nipples, already standing to attention beneath his appreciative inspection, tightened still more when he leaned forward to tease them with the tip of his tongue. She was so sensitive that when he drew the first bud into the heat of his mouth and laved it with his tongue she had to try again to make contact and bucked beneath him, not caring what he thought of her. But Shahin had left his hands free to press her down, to control her, to hold her steady while he prepared her for what was to come next. And when she was reduced to sobbing with pleasure he silenced her cries with a kiss.

And now the longing to touch him, to please him had grown stronger inside her. She wanted to weave her fingers through his hair and keep him close. 'Release me,' she commanded the moment their lips parted.

'I will, after this…'

Zara couldn't believe the sensation when Shahin began to stroke her belly and, with a sharp cry, she ground her hips against the bed. Fire raced through her veins as his fingers teased her—fire that ended in a feather-touch of warmth that caressed each nerve-ending as she bucked mindlessly beneath him in the hunt for a more intimate assault.

Shahin's answer was to dip his fingers beneath the waistband of her briefs, searching, teasing, but never quite reaching the place she wanted him to be. But then he removed his hand and, with studied deliberation, opened the fastening on her trousers and laid them wide.

'Take them off,' Zara instructed him, lifting her hips from the bed.

Shahin laughed softly, but he did as she asked. 'And now?' he demanded, staring into her eyes.

Lacing her fingers through his hair, she whispered, 'And now you kiss me…'

'And how is that?'

'Like this…' Drawing him to her, she teased the seam of his mouth with her tongue and then planted a soft kiss on his bottom lip. 'And like this…' Another on his top lip… 'And like this…' She softly captured the full swell of his bottom lip between her teeth. 'And finally…like this.' Angling her head, she slipped her tongue into his mouth. As their tongues clashed, she sucked on his shamelessly, delighting in it, shivering with arousal as Shahin clasped her in his arms.

'And now?' he prompted, humour glinting in his eyes.

'Don't pretend you don't know…'

'But I'm enjoying my lesson,' he complained huskily.

And so she gave him the next lesson, drawing his robe slowly up his body—until her bluff was called and she stopped abruptly.

'Does it surprise you that I wear nothing beneath my robe?' Shahin demanded with amusement.

She couldn't stop staring at his arousal, but somehow managed to drag her gaze away. 'Nothing would surprise me about you,' she offered boldly.

'It is much more comfortable to go commando in the desert.'

'I'm sure it is. And much more convenient, perhaps?'

'Of course,' he agreed.

Tumbling her on to her back, Shahin moved into the dominant position. Slipping his hands down beneath her briefs, he cupped her buttocks. Zara gave a little cry of excitement, but he hadn't finished with her yet. Parting the softly yielding cheeks, he released them… And then, just when she was thinking she couldn't be more aroused and that he couldn't expect her to sustain this level of stimulation a moment longer, he did it again…

'I hate you,' she panted feverishly. 'You're too cruel—'

'I know,' Shahin whispered against her mouth.

But his eyes were dancing with laughter, Zara noticed as he used his thumbs to stroke and tease her thighs apart. 'I can't stand it…'

'Yes, you can,' Shahin insisted, kissing away her sobs of frustration, 'and you must…'

'Then you must allow me to undress you…' She didn't wait for his reply. Grabbing the edge of his robe, she tugged it over his head.

And gulped. His body was as stunning as she remembered… Only this time she saw that his belly was as hard and well muscled as his torso. He glowed with vigour and with strength like polished copper in the lamplight. She was careful to edit her inspection, not sure she was ready for a second look. And then she felt a flicker of fear seeing the power in his thighs… Would he be too big for her? Too demanding? *Would she disappoint him?*

Reaching up to safer ground, she ran her fingers lightly over the wide spread of his shoulders and on again down his arms. She wanted to tease Shahin as much as he had teased her. She found his nipples and toyed with them, pleased to hear him sigh, pleased to feel them harden as she nipped them between her thumb and forefinger.

Shahin pulled away. 'And so you want to play games with me?'

'It's only fair,' Zara pointed out. She felt so small against him, so helpless. And yet when Shahin groaned beneath her hands she felt so strong. When he sighed, when he was forced to pull away because he couldn't bear the level of pleasure she was giving him, she wanted to deal out more of it.

She wanted more of him. And then she remembered the first time, remembered tasting him…

Pressing Shahin down on the bed, Zara ran her hand over his flat belly. Closing her eyes so the sight of him fully aroused would do nothing to deter her, she brushed her hands against him. She found him as she had expected, thick, hard and pulsating beneath her touch. His groan made her smile and grow in confidence. She could feel him becoming harder and starting to flex beneath her touch. It was impossible not to think about that delicious action occurring inside her. It took both her hands to encompass his girth now and as she gripped him she had to wait a moment in order to gain courage enough to explore further… And then she traced his length, from the nest of springing curls to the silky tip so beautifully formed, so perfect for slipping inside her…

'Do I please you?' he murmured.

She couldn't possibly tell him how much. 'Yes, you do…' But she was coming to believe that he was far too big for her. But she wanted him so badly… And then her mouth closed over him and she tasted him. It thrilled her to feel him thrusting deeper into her moist, silky warmth. She wanted to please him, but she was frightened too. Now the moment of truth was here she was frightened of Shahin possessing her as a man must possess a woman. But this was a way to please them both, Zara convinced herself. And she loved the taste of him, the texture of him beneath her tongue, the strength, the power, the raised veins that pulsed with life...

'Are you frightened of me?' Drawing back, Shahin lifted her up the bed. 'Zara?' He made the whispered demand staring into her eyes so she had no escape. 'Do you believe I would hurt you?'

Her eyes filled with tears as she stared at him. He knew so much about her. But maybe there was something else holding him back. 'Did I do something wrong?' Her cheeks burned beneath his scrutiny, but then warmth flooded through her when she saw the tenderness in his eyes.

'You did nothing wrong... But something tells me you're drawing back, you're postponing the moment when—'

'No, I—' Placing her finger across his lips, she shook her head. But Shahin quickly took hold of her hand and kissed her palm.

'I understand,' he whispered. Drawing her down beside him in the bed, he stroked her and soothed her until she began to respond, slowly at first, but then with increasing ardour as her body cried out for his touch.

'If you want me to stop,' he murmured, 'you only have to tell me that you've changed your mind.'

To each of the questions in his eyes she answered no. There was such warmth and such tenderness in Shahin's eyes and she held his stare until she knew that he was no longer in any doubt in his mind that her resolve was fixed.

'Then shall I prepare you?' He drew her excited gasp into his mouth, kissing her deeply as he cupped the swollen mound between her legs over the cobweb fabric of her briefs. His fingers strayed a little, but never enough, and he always managed to evade her best attempts to lure him on.

As he stripped off her briefs she moved eagerly to help him. She had no inhibitions left that had not been overtaken by hunger. She wanted him so badly she drew her knees back in anticipation and, locking her hands behind Shahin's waist, closed her eyes.

Zara cried out softly, not sure that she could survive the pleasure, as Shahin delicately began to touch her most sensitive place.

'Is that good?'

Shahin didn't need an answer as she moved beneath him. He heard her sighs and saw the pleasure he was giving her reflected in her eyes. But she wanted to please him too. 'Make love to me, Shahin... I want you so badly. Oh, please, Shahin, I love—'

He cut her off with a kiss and absorbed the cry she made as he entered her. He moved slowly to possess her in the most sensitive way she could have imagined...

'Am I hurting you?'

The truth was he would have hurt her more had he stopped. Her answer was to rock back on her hips, affording him greater access.

Cupping her face in his hands, Shahin kissed her deeply, tangling his tongue with hers before plunging into the dark secret warmth of her mouth. He stopped once briefly when she cried out. But the moment soon passed and her eyes cleared again.

'Are you all right?' he demanded huskily, dropping kisses on her eyelids.

'Please...' It was the one word she could manage, the

only word that perfectly expressed her wishes, and so he moved deeper until her muscles closed around him and he inhabited her completely.

And then at last he moved, side to side without withdrawing, rolling gently to massage the very place that had waited so long for his attention. She couldn't hold back, she didn't want to… She had become greedy for him, greedy for Shahin and all the pleasure she knew he could bring her. She thrust her pelvis against him, grinding hungrily, so incredibly aware and sensitive… She didn't even hear herself calling out for satisfaction—ordering him, begging him, because her heart was thundering so loudly in her ears. Her skin was warm and her fingers dug into him, into his buttocks, driving him, encouraging him… And then light enveloped her, exploding in her head in a starburst of sensation that left her oblivious to her surroundings. And then, as she slowly grew conscious again to those things that existed outside the pleasure vortex, Shahin began to move.

He thrust steadily, bringing her with him, raising himself on stiff arms so he could watch the pleasure unfolding on her face. Growing accustomed to his rhythm, she rose to meet him, moving with him, working her hips to draw him deeper, while his warm hands cupped her buttocks to support her and hold her in place. She responded eagerly as he pleasured her, catching hold of him and then splaying her fingers against his chest as he moved faster. She wanted every inch of her to be in contact with Shahin, but he misread the signal and, taking it as a warning sign, drew back.

'I just want to feel every part of you,' Zara reassured him.

His lips tugged up in a smile. 'Like this?' he suggested, moving deep. As she groaned with pleasure he withdrew so that it was like starting over again when he took her the next time. And then he wouldn't stop teasing her and made her wait a little longer and a little longer for each new assault until she was thrashing helplessly beneath him.

'Don't tease me, Shahin—' Taking hold of his hips, Zara showed him clearly what she wanted.

'Like this, then…' He set up a fast pace that had her gasping with pleasure and surprise.

'Oh, yes…yes…' She clung on as he thrust over and over, building up the pleasure until she knew it had to find an outlet again. She heard someone wailing with anticipation, calling out excitedly, someone moaning rhythmically and making guttural animal sounds down low in her throat, sounds that rang to a primitive beat until the world and everything in it dissolved once again into pleasure.

'I don't think I need to ask if you enjoyed that,' Shahin murmured against her ear. 'In fact, I only have one question for you…'

'And what's that?' Turning her face up lazily, she looked at him.

'More?'

With a wanton sigh Zara wrapped her legs around his waist.

CHAPTER ELEVEN

IT WAS only necessary to give the slightest indication with his thighs for Jal to respond. Plunging forward eagerly, ears pricked, the stallion's polished hooves pounded the sand, eating up the distance between the encampment and the mountains beyond the plain. It would take an hour of hard riding for him to get there, an hour in which to excise his demons...

Leaning low over Jal's neck, Shahin pressed him on. By the time they arrived at the source of the underground stream where Jal could drink and rest in preparation for the homeward journey, he had to be ready to face facts.

And find an answer?

With a fierce sound, Shahin loosened the reins, allowing the horse his head; he didn't expect a miracle.

The moment they arrived he sprang down and went to break off fistfuls of the coarse, dry grass that somehow managed to survive in the shadow of the granite outcrop. The horse's dark hide was flecked with sweat and, bunching the grass, he rubbed him down vigorously. He hadn't wasted time on a saddle, but a fiery horse like Jal was better ridden with a bridle, or like a wayward woman would rush heedlessly into danger...

No one could accuse Zara of being wayward, Shahin reflected grimly. In fact, she was anything but. She had hidden her inner passion beneath a cloak of good sense and caution, and it was he who had shown her another path, a dangerous path, an erotic path...

Picking up the reins, Shahin began walking the horse, talking to him soothingly as Jal snorted his impatience to reach the water. 'Not yet,' Shahin whispered in one quivering ear, pulling the forelock out of his stallion's eyes. 'First you must cool down...'

As he paced with the horse, Shahin wondered if he could despise himself more. It wasn't the fact that Zara was his ward that troubled him, for as she had pointed out that problem was not insurmountable. There were precedents for relationships and even marriages between ward and guardian. It was that having discovered a beautiful and inviolate flower he had trampled it underfoot. Desire had blinded him to duty, to moral scruples—he hadn't given a thought to what would happen next. But the future had hit him in the face when he had woken to find her sleeping at his side. He had known then that he could not allow the susceptibilities of a man to interfere with the duties of a king.

In other countries a man might marry a princess, or a prince a secretary, but in Zaddara such a thing was unthinkable. The ruling sheikh must marry someone appropriate—a virgin from a neighbouring territory in an arrangement that would bring benefits to both parties. That was what he had decided he would do long before he had met Zara Kingston. Privilege came with a price and his account had just fallen due.

'Shahin?' Feeling the empty space on the bed beside her, Zara opened her eyes. Thin strands of sunlight were spilling into the pavilion, falling in silver streaks across the bed. At first she thought dawn must be rising over the desert and she was waking in good time for the dreaded riding lesson, but then she realised that the heavy silk curtains were still drawn and only fingers of light were seeping through.

Sitting up, she looked around and then stayed still to listen. She hoped to hear the shower running or the sound of strong limbs plying the cool waters of the private pool. But she was alone and the silence was heavy and complete.

Her body, still languid from sleep, was throbbing from the effects of so much lovemaking. Thinking about Shahin made her smile and, tugging off one of the sheets, she wrapped it tightly round her naked body and slipped out of bed to go and look for him.

Padding across the cool floor to the double doors leading on to the veranda, she opened them and paused a moment to enjoy the gust of warm air that greeted her. She couldn't believe she had slept so long. It must be almost noon, she guessed, gazing up into a flawless cobalt sky.

Her discarded clothes were still strewn across the floor like an obstacle course, she noticed with amusement, picking her way around them for a second time. Flinging herself down in contentment on to the tangle of silk and satin covers, she caught sight of her reflection in the mirrored canopy. Her cheeks flushed red as she remembered... But where was Shahin?

He had left nothing behind him in the room, Zara noticed. It was as if he had never been there at all and she had imagined everything... Was that what he wanted her to think? Her stomach clenched with anxiety as she thought about it... But then the sound of a horse's hooves brought the smile back to her face and, slipping off the bed, she hurried back to the open door.

Feeling a rush of excitement as she identified the horse and rider, Zara knew what must have happened. When she hadn't woken at dawn as they had agreed, Shahin had gone riding without her. Being considerate, he hadn't wanted to wake her....

Walking out on to the veranda, she shaded her eyes and waved, secretly glad that she had missed her first riding lesson. She would only have held them back, Zara reflected, admiring the way Shahin rode the stallion as if he were part of the horse.

Jal was walking at a steady pace as horse and rider approached the encampment. Thanks to Shahin's concern for the animal, Zara thought. It was hot now and Shahin would never overwork his horse. He must have left very early to give the stallion such a good workout, she realised, seeing Jal's usually glossy hide was coated in dust.

Hurrying inside to shower and make herself presentable, Zara found it hard to contain her excitement. She couldn't wait to be with Shahin again. Their relationship had changed irrevocably and she only had to remember the look in his eyes when he'd held her in his arms for the thrill of desire to return.

She couldn't wait to tell Shahin how much he meant to her when they fell into each other's arms. That would give him the opportunity to confide that he felt the same... He always held back when it came to expressing his feelings, but today she felt confident that all he would need was a tiny push.

He had been so gentle with her, so loving and passionate, and in return she had given him everything. Shahin had made her first experience of lovemaking beautiful... Though, looking back, she could see that she had tensed at the crucial moment and might have spoiled it for him.

She would be able to reassure him about that too and tell him it had been everything she had hoped for and more... She couldn't wait.

From the moment Shahin entered the room Zara was filled with a sense of foreboding. Had he left her to sleep or simply decided to leave her? The expression on his face made her think the latter might be the more likely explanation.

He stood by the door with his whip and riding gloves in his hand, as if to emphasise the fact that this would only be a short visit. She might be naïve, but she wasn't naïve enough to think that he had come straight from the stables because he couldn't wait to see her. His body language assured her that wasn't the case. No. He was impatient to get whatever he had come to say to her over and done with. He must have woken at her side and regretted everything that had happened. Her dream had been Shahin's nightmare...

Shivering a little, she forced herself to meet his gaze. Everything she hoped not to see was in his eyes. He had enjoyed her and he would never forgive himself for that. And, quite possibly, he believed she had led him on...

What could she do? She would not feel ashamed and she did not regret what had happened. So should she give in without a fight? As he stared at her she felt as if a huge gulf had widened between them. And the feeling made her all the more determined to prove him wrong. She hadn't come all this way in her feelings for him to turn back now. She wasn't a coward and she wouldn't run from love. Why would she, when she had been searching for love all her life?

She would tell him how she felt and that she understood his reservations. It was up to her to put their feelings into words. Shahin's life had been channelled into duty and maintaining his dignity, which made it impossible for him to express his emotions freely. She understood that and she also understood that reserve like his couldn't be broken down all at once. Everything would be right again when she told Shahin how much she loved him…

'What are you saying, Zara?' As he looked at her and saw the love shining from her eyes, he wondered how he could ever have imagined his guilt could be mitigated by a taxing ride. It had just come flooding back, only now it was redoubled.

Confidence radiated from her as she told him again, 'I love you…'

The honesty blazing from her eyes emphasised how young she was, how innocent. He should have anticipated this because, however wise she appeared, however strong and determined, she was inexperienced in every way. For all her talk of independence, of carving a life for herself, she was unworldly, and he had taken advantage of that fact and had ridden roughshod over her dreams. And now, at the very moment when she declared her love for him, he must abuse her trust in him one last time.

'You mustn't say that,' he murmured gently, removing her hands from his shoulders. She had laid her head on his chest so trustingly he felt ashamed. But, whatever she had conjured in her mind, this was the moment when he must kill her hopes once and for all.

'I know you find it difficult to say what's in your heart,' she said, staring up at him, refusing to acknowledge the coolness in his gaze.

'Zara, please… Don't make this any harder than it has to be.'

'What do you mean?' The glow lasted for barely an instant and then abruptly it vanished and her face crumpled. 'Don't you want me, Shahin?'

'You know I do…' He turned away to gather his thoughts. He had been conveniently blind to how vulnerable she was, but now he had to face the fact that he had slept with her and that he shouldn't have and that, having been the first, he had taken something from her that could never be restored.

There was only one way he could help her now and that was to convince her that she was better off without him in any romantic sense and that a working arrangement, along with a strict guardian/ward relationship was the most she could expect. 'Of course I want to be with you,' he said with a false air of optimism. 'We're going to be working together, aren't we? But—'

'But?'

Her gaze was razor-sharp and she picked up his meaning fast. Her eyes might hold hurt, pain and disillusionment, but she would not be lightly dismissed. She had hoped for so much more than he could give her, but that didn't mean she was a fool. 'But… You must see that an intimate relationship between us can never work,' he said plainly.

'Oh,' she said thoughtfully, as if she might be giving some consideration to his words.

He drove on. 'You'd have a poor life with me, Zara… I'm bound by duty; I'm not free to follow my own inclinations—'

'As you did last night…'

She spoke so gently he didn't take it as a warning and, in his desire to avoid revisiting anything to do with the passionate night they'd spent together, he gave a humourless laugh. 'You'd be miserable as my wife.'

'Your wife?' Her surprise was obvious. And then another expression came into her eyes: disbelief, rapidly followed by contempt that he should, out of desperation or a desire to be rid of her, place what *might have been* on so high a level.

'Yes, I respect you too much to…' He hunted for the right words, words they might both find acceptable. *To make you my mistress* felt wrong, sordid under these circumstances.

But before he had the chance to finish the sentence she demanded, 'Don't you feel anything for me, Shahin?' Her eyes were full of tears, but her tone was angry.

'Of course I do. But—'

'But?' She cut across him passionately as if she loathed the word. 'Have I just made a complete fool of myself, Shahin?'

'No, of course you haven't!'

'I think I have,' she said stubbornly.

'Zara, you must know that what we have is—'

'What?' she said, cutting across him coldly.

'Well, it's wonderful.'

'Wonderful?'

'But it can't go anywhere. Can it?' he demanded gently, appealing to her common sense. 'You know the position I'm in—'

'Would that be your position as ruling Sheikh of Zaddara, your position as my guardian, or your position in my bed? You'll have to excuse me here, Shahin—' She clutched her arms as she shook her head. 'Only I'm getting a little confused—'

'Don't do this to yourself.' He reached out to her, but she pulled away.

'What? What am I doing to myself, Shahin? Am I facing up to the truth, perhaps?'

'It doesn't have to be like this—'

'So how should it be? What was I for you, Shahin? A workout? Part of your exercise regime? What? Where do I fit into your life?'

'Don't talk like that, Zara. Don't demean yourself—'

'Demean myself?' she scoffed. 'You're doing a pretty good job of that without my help.'

'Zara, please—'

She knocked his hand off her shoulder. 'Is this how guardians behave in Zaddara? Before I got here I guessed your country might be behind the times, but I never dreamt the ruling sheikh would still exercise *droit de seigneur!* Do you make a habit of trying out all the available virgins, or am I the first of this new reign? Well?'

Tears were streaming down her face, making her look more vulnerable than ever.

'Answer me, damn you!' she railed at him.

'What did you think would come of this? You must have known you couldn't stay here long-term. What would you be? What would you do?' The blood drained from her face as he hammered each of the nails into the coffin holding her dreams. 'And you were right,' he admitted, 'you could never be my wife. And it's unthinkable that you would be my mistress—'

'No, I suppose I couldn't be both your mistress and your ward,' she observed scathingly. 'But one day you will marry, Shahin.' She bit down on her lip and it took her a moment to gather her thoughts again. And then she said bitterly, 'You will have to take a wife, if only to continue the royal line—'

The way she said 'royal' made it sound like some aberrant strain of human being.

'The woman who agrees to be my wife will have to be an exceptional human being,' he conceded. 'The responsibility alone will be stifling…' He hoped she would see that he couldn't possibly subject a free spirit like Zara to a life sentence of duty and protocol. He looked at her again, beseeching her with his eyes to understand as he waited for her to react, to say something…

'Your wife…' She went white. And, rather than rail at him, she covered her mouth with her hand and everything she was feeling inside poured out. 'I won't be able to bear it…'

That she could be so open with him after everything they'd said to each other shocked him. She had so much raw emotion inside her and there was no self-belief or inborn arrogance to hold it in. He longed to help her, to comfort her, but when he tried to touch her, her hand shot up to ward him off.

'You have no idea what marriage to a man like me would involve—'

'Oh, no?'

He watched the strength pour back into her tear-stained face.

'Wouldn't it involve love and laughter and children, Shahin? Wouldn't it involve working together, side by side, for the good of the people of Zaddara? Don't shake your head at me, Shahin. It's you who needs help. You're more damaged than you know. You may be a giant of a man, a sheikh who is wealthy beyond imagining, but you're poor inside. In here—' she punched her chest '—you're emotionally dead!'

'Don't be ridiculous, you're overreacting—'

'Oh, I'm being ridiculous?' Shaking her head, she smiled, but it was a sad smile. 'You're the one who's being ridiculous, Shahin. You're not capable of love and you can't see that what that means is that you have nothing to offer your people. Yes, they want duty, but they want your love too. People need love, Shahin. No one understands that better than me.'

He was stunned by what she had said, but even so he had to let her go. And the only way he could drive this to a conclusion was by withdrawing from her and by standing on his dignity. 'Unfortunately, Zara, you're too young to know the difference between a schoolgirl crush and love.' He controlled himself with difficulty as a fresh stream of tears poured down her face. He willed her to be angry with him, to lose control, to express her hatred for him, but instead she was suddenly quite composed.

'I think we both know I'm all grown up, Shahin,' she said softly.

She had collected herself with such strength of will he flinched in the face of her sad reproach.

'Don't you think I've waited long enough for love to know love when I find it?' she said.

Her honesty was so brutal he couldn't fail to be moved by it, but as he pushed caution aside and went to take hold of her to comfort her, she shook him off.

'Don't...touch...me!'

'Zara, don't do this...' He followed her across the room and stood watching in silence as she started stuffing her clothes into a bag.

'I'm already doing it, Shahin. All you have to do is find someone to take me back to the capital. I'm flying out of Zaddara the first chance I get. I take it you can organise that much for me without it trespassing on your precious pride?'

'Of course I can...' For the first time in his life he was at a loss to know how to stop events rolling forward without his guiding hand deciding which direction they would take. 'But what about the exhibition?' He was willing to pull out all the stops to slow things down. 'What about the work we planned here in Zaddara? What about the memorial to your parents?' As she flashed him a glance he knew it was a cheap shot. And she didn't let it pass her by.

'The memorial to my parents?' Lifting her head, she stared at him and he saw then the full extent of the damage he'd done. Hurt brown eyes shamed him as she pressed her hand against her chest. 'The memorial to my parents is in here, Shahin. I don't know why I didn't see that all along.'

'But we have a chance to build something special in

Zaddara, something that will stand as a memorial to my father, as well as to your parents, a living monument that will show their struggle—'

He was wasting his time. She was looking at him as though he were mad to think they could ever work together now. But conceding defeat wasn't a concept he recognised. 'We have a chance to create a gallery of images that will stand as a guiding principle for all the young people of Zaddara—'

'You still think of me as one of those "young people", don't you, Shahin? You can't see that life makes some people grow up faster than others. You don't understand that some of us must take on responsibility at a much younger age than other people because we have no choice... And that it doesn't mean we need your pity,' she raged in case he hadn't got the message.

The look she gave him spoke of the childhood that had been stolen from her and the way she had rebuilt her life without anybody's help.

He had to mend bridges and fast. 'I thought—'

'You thought you'd talk to me about guiding principles and I'd be pacified. You thought if you made me see the bigger picture everything would be okay. But I do see the bigger picture and it's still not okay.'

'So what about our gallery?'

'*Your* gallery, Shahin. The Zaddaran gallery of historic images where, no doubt, I'd always be a welcome visitor.'

'Of course you'd be welcome. How could you not be welcome when most of the work will be yours and the rest of it your parents'—' He stopped as she frowned. A bad feeling was growing in the pit of his stomach.

'That's something else we have to talk about. As far as my parents' things are concerned, I want to have them shipped home to England. I presume that even you wouldn't deny me that much?'

He needed time to think how to get round this. And found none. 'If that's what you want?'

'It is.'

There was nothing left him but the authority card, which he now played. 'You're right, we do have to talk about this before you make any rash decisions—'

'I'm not being rash, Shahin, I've made up my mind. We just did all the talking we're going to do—and they're coming home with me.'

'You're still my ward. You'll need my authority to remove them from Zaddara.'

'In that case…' She remained quite calm. 'I think I should also tell you that the collection you bought at the exhibition is no longer for sale.'

'But I already bought them. The shipping is arranged.'

'Then un-arrange it. The exhibits aren't for sale. I just took them off the market.'

'You can't do that—'

'I just did.' And then everything she was holding back welled up in her eyes. 'The artist changed her mind, Shahin. Fickle, women, aren't they?'

His jaw worked as he fielded the verbal jab. 'But I've already paid for all the pieces in your collection.'

'Your money will be returned to you in full.'

'By Gideon and Lambert?' His voice hardened.

Zara faltered momentarily. She hadn't taken account of her sponsors, he guessed.

'I'll talk to them,' she said finally.

Her voice was dry and he guessed she was calculating the amount of money it would take to buy them off. Gideon and Lambert levied a sizeable commission on anything sold in their gallery—and that didn't include the generous mark-up they added to the 'for their eyes only' price list. He was willing to bet Zara would receive less than a tenth of what he'd paid for her exhibits by the time the wily gallery owners had finished deducting for this and that. Whatever his personal feelings, he couldn't stand by and see her fleeced. 'Very well… I have no wish to keep them if you feel so strongly about them, but maybe I should handle that side of things for you.'

'How would you do that?' she asked him suspiciously.

'I'll make sure the exhibits are released into your hands and compensation paid to the gallery. What?' He had expected her to be grateful, reassured even, but now she looked more worried than ever. And then he remembered how small her apartment was and that some of her exhibits were over twelve feet tall. 'Perhaps I could ask my people in London to find you an exhibition hall—'

She gave a humourless laugh.

'Okay, I guess that won't be easy, but we'll think of something else…' At least she was listening. 'There's always the embassy—' He had to admit to a flush of pleasure as he thought of it, because now she was looking at him with real interest. 'You have a substantial fan base,' he went on. 'And I dare say a change of venue from hip gallery to an exotic eastern location conveniently located in the centre of London would bring people flocking to the exhibition.'

She was in no hurry to dispute any of the points he'd raised, Shahin realised thankfully, and so he pressed for a conclusion. 'What do you think?'

What did she think? That Shahin was more securely locked in the past than she was. That he refused to accept that at twenty she'd had more life experience than many people twice her age. That they loved each other. She was utterly confident on that point, but again, he couldn't or wouldn't accept it. Shahin needed somebody strong and resourceful to stand at his side, but he wouldn't see that she would work tirelessly in the service of the country he loved, the country her parents had loved and the only place, she had begun to realise since seeing where her parents had lived, that she might ever have a chance of calling home.

Could she forget everything that had happened between them in order to house her work? Or should she harbour a grudge against Shahin and throw her career into jeopardy? He had offered her a way out of her immediate difficulties and if she could remove emotion from the equation it should be possible to go forward from this with her head held high. 'Thank you... That's a very generous offer; I'd like to take you up on it.'

CHAPTER TWELVE

ZARA had quickly come to think of the Zaddaran embassy as a haven of warmth and welcome in the heart of chilly London. Considering her history with the country's ruler, that was quite an accolade. Muffled up to the nose in scarf and jacket, she slipped inside the heavy front door, acknowledging the security man with a bright smile. But beneath it she was worried. The year was drawing to a close and with it her tenure on the embassy ballroom. She couldn't complain; she'd had use of the ballroom for well over a month, but her exhibition would have to be removed to make room for the concerts that were always a highlight of the London holiday season.

As ruling sheikh Shahin would be arriving soon to act as host for the festivities… Zara couldn't pretend she hadn't looked over her shoulder every day since the first of her exhibits had gone up in the hope that he might walk into the ballroom and surprise her. There was nothing subtle in the way she felt about him. He'd hurt her and discarded her, but love like she felt for Shahin wouldn't conveniently go away and, no matter how many times she told herself that it was wasted on a man who couldn't see beyond his duty to a country, her love for him remained undiminished.

Did he ever think about her? Zara wondered as a smiling attendant took her scarf and coat. Did the Sheikh of Zaddara feel the same sense of loss she did, or had Shahin simply shut her out of his mind?

She would never know. And now she had to make arrangements for her exhibition to be stored somewhere else, which would cut a huge chunk out of her budget and leave her wildlife charities without the level of funding they required. But before she turned her mind to that problem she had one last chance to walk around her exhibition and enjoy it before the general public were admitted.

Shahin hesitated outside the ornate doors leading into the embassy ballroom, knowing he should have stayed away. He should have waited another few days and then she would have been gone. But he couldn't resist seeing what she had done with the exhibits. Or at least that was his excuse for being in London a week early. The truth was, he couldn't stay away. And now he was dithering in front of one of his advisors like a youth who didn't know his own mind.

'How long has she been in there?' His voice was firm as he turned to his aide-de-camp in London. He was playing for time, steeling himself. Preparing to see her again after all this time wasn't as easy as he had imagined. She was unpredictable; she could always surprise him; he had no idea how she would greet him.

'Not long, sir. Perhaps twenty minutes…'

Twenty minutes on her own… What was she thinking, remembering? 'Thank you… That's all…' Shahin sensed, rather than saw his aide bow and then back away discreetly leaving him alone. Easing his neck in the immaculately starched white collar, he sucked in a steadying breath before opening the door.

She was standing in the centre of the dance floor with her back to him. The scale of the room made her seem smaller, more fragile than ever. She wore a calf-length skirt with boots and a roll-neck sweater—all in black, as if she were in mourning, and her hair fell loose in a glimmering cascade to her waist. She looked as young as ever, and just as vulnerable.

She remained absolutely still, though she must have heard the door open. He wished he could see her face… But he could see how stiff her shoulders had suddenly become and how rigid her back.

She knew it was him… 'Zara…'

Her shoulders eased as he spoke, almost as if she had been expecting him, and then she turned and all the tension he had expected to see in her face drained away. Her eyes glowed with love and her smile lit up the room. She came towards him with her hands outstretched, as honest and as open in her feelings towards him as she had ever been.

'Hello, Shahin…'

When he first heard her voice again, speaking his name, he couldn't put his feelings into words. She transformed him—her lack of guile, the omission of any rebuke or bitterness in her tone, when she had every reason to hate him for what he'd done to her. 'Zara…' Taking her hands in his, he raised them to his lips. And then, because he couldn't resist forces stronger than himself, he took her in his arms and held her close.

'Can I show you round?' she asked, staring up into his eyes when he finally released her.

Her composure, her absolute certainty that he would come to see her exhibition, her trust in him, her sincerity touched him, shamed him, made him face up to the fact that he loved her beyond anything else in his existence. 'I'd like that…'

His throat was raw from holding back his feelings by the time he had completed the circuit of her exhibits. He had never been so deeply moved. She had enlarged all the early photographs of her parents with his father… And they were young again, their faces full of confidence and laughter in the midst of all their struggles. There was no sign of her father's alcoholism in any of the images, and for that he was eternally grateful and had cause again to be glad that he hadn't told her everything he might have. All he could see in those old prints was youthful fire and zest for life… It had all been theirs and she had brought it back to life again. Her love for his country showed in every image. All the artefacts that had been rescued from the old cabin were beautifully displayed, with carefully thought out notes to explain their provenance…

'Do you like it?'

'Like it?' His voice sounded tight. 'You've done a great job…' *A great job?* Was that the best he could come up with?

'It's been a sell-out. We've raised thousands for Zaddaran charities.'

'You've raised thousands,' he corrected her. 'And I can't thank you enough…' He sounded so stiff, so formal.

'Don't thank me…' She laughed. 'You gave my exhibition a home, remember?'

'Still, I would like you to accept my thanks…'

'Of course…' She stared into his eyes.

'And so…'

'And so?' she pressed, still smiling.

'I'd like you to have dinner with me,' he blurted, wondering at his sudden loss of assurance. The thought that she might well refuse him was frightening.

'With my guardian?'

She needed clarification. He owed her that much. 'Will my ward accept?'

There was the smallest flicker of adjustment in her gaze, but she quickly recovered. 'It would mean a lot to me if we could part as friends, Shahin.'

'Yes…' He gathered himself. 'Me, too.'

They didn't go out to a restaurant that evening, but at Shahin's invitation ate dinner in his apartment at the embassy, which played into her hands. It was quiet and private in the wood-panelled sitting room. The muted masculine colours, deep-cushioned seating and roaring fire made everything cosy, Zara thought with approval, looking round. It was smaller than she had expected, but perfect. 'This is lovely…'

'I'm glad you think so… And I hope you're hungry.' Glancing at the feast that had been laid out for them, Shahin smiled.

'Starving.'

He had no idea, Zara thought, keeping her expression strictly neutral.

As always, Shahin looked magnificent in his flowing black robes and she knew enough about him now to know that, apart from the trousers secured only by a loosely tied drawstring, he would be naked underneath.

Swallowing hard, she had to accept that since meeting Shahin both diplomacy and caution, once her strong points, had been thrown to the wind. And, having decided on a plan of action, it was time to put it into effect. 'Will we be disturbed?' she asked innocently.

Shahin's face grew serious. 'I hope you know that if you ever need to speak to me in private, Zara—about anything,' he emphasised earnestly, 'you only have to ask.'

'I'm asking…' She tried to look as if she had something really serious on her mind.

'Go on,' he encouraged, sitting forward so she had a great view down the slashed neck of his robe to the hard bronzed body underneath.

'What is it, Zara?'

His voice was deliciously cajoling and filled her with conviction that she was doing the right thing. 'It's not easy…' She bit her lip.

Holding her gaze, Shahin picked up the phone.

'What are you doing?' Zara couldn't believe she was managing to keep the shake out of her voice.

'Making sure we're not disturbed—' Turning from her, he rapped out a few words in Zaddaran.

'Thank you…' She had to clench her fists at her sides to keep from laughing. Her plan was unfolding without her having to do a thing. If it all went so well…

'Now,' Shahin said, smiling reassurance, 'Why don't you tell me what's worrying you…?'

If you won't change, then once again I shall have to make you, Zara thought, holding his gaze. There's your answer, Shahin. So perhaps it's you who should be worried, because I don't have a cut-off point where I give up. I never had anyone to teach me how to accept defeat, which is quite a bonus when you think about it. 'It's a little involved…' She sighed.

'I'm listening…'

Shahin sat back to show her how relaxed he was. But that didn't last long. 'Zara, what are you doing?' He shot up, his amazed gaze following her hands as she stood and swept off her lacy cardigan.

Her breasts were accentuated in the tight-fitting top she wore underneath. 'Don't you think it's a little hot in here, Shahin?'

He couldn't look away, which was good, and so she smoothed her hands down over her body from her breasts to her waist, and then on over her hips and finally her thighs. Easing her neck, she levelled a gaze at him and found him motionless, staring at her, mesmerised.

'I could open a window if you're too warm,' he suggested faintly.

'That won't be necessary. Hot is good…'

That moment, as Shahin stared at her in silence and she couldn't read his mind, was the longest moment of her life.

They came together like an elemental force—the need to touch, to feel, to kiss, to possess, overwhelming every rational thought for both of them. Shahin had her clothes off in moments and Zara made short work of his.

Holding her to him, Shahin backed her towards the fur rug in front of the fire. But she couldn't wait to get there and, throwing her arms around his neck, she sprang up and wrapped her legs around his waist, leaning back so he had no alternative but to do as she demanded. Sinking deep with an animal roar, it was Shahin's turn to throw his head back in ecstasy as she closed her muscles around him and held him tight.

'You're mine,' she told him fiercely. And then she moved her hips with strong, deliberate thrusts, daring him to argue.

'Good…so good,' Shahin moaned, allowing Zara to dictate the pace. Completely naked, he stood firm in the middle of the room, supporting her weight with his strong hands clamped around her buttocks as she took him firmly and deeply, over and over again, driving them both to the peak of ecstasy. He cried out first and then she followed an instant later.

He had lost control. He had never done that before. Not once. And never like this. But he was shaken to the core. Kissing her gently, he inhaled the fragrance of her hair, wondering how he had lived without her sweetness. Laying her down gently on the soft fur rug, he sank into her as if they had been lovers for ever. She was so small and yet they fitted together so well, and they already knew that this was something neither of them had the power to resist.

'You're mine, Shahin… Mine,' she gasped, clinging to his arms as he pleasured her.

He didn't doubt it. She was a lioness, a queen, and the only mother he could ever want for his children…

'I want your child, Shahin…' She looked straight into his eyes as if she had a window into his soul. 'Fill me, make me yours…'

His answer was to kiss her deeply, slowing the pace of their lovemaking so that she could feel the depth of his love for her first. The desire to make love to her, really make love to her, was overwhelming. They would never be parted again. That was a vow he made to himself and would make to Zara in every way he knew. They would stay together always—that was what both destiny *and* his heart had decreed.

But for now… She was already grinding against him, asking for more. Cupping him, she nursed him, stroking him into a frenzy of desire. He was her slave and could only thrust deeper and faster in response to her coaxing, and only just managed to hold back when he saw the look of astonishment in her eyes that always marked the first wave of her climax. She clung to him, bucking convulsively as he found his own savage release, and when she softened against him this time he found it was his eyes that had filled with tears.

An ironic half-smile touched his lips as she looked at him, and when he saw the wonder and sheer exhilaration in her eyes he confirmed, 'Yes, emotion… Something new for me.'

'Something new for the man who has everything?' she teased him gently.

'I had nothing before I had you,' he assured her fiercely, his voice thickening.

'It's very lonely at the top of the mountain, isn't it, Shahin?'

'Not any longer,' he said, capturing her hand as she stroked his face. Pressing a kiss against her palm, he smiled deep into her eyes. 'I think I've found someone who can bring me down to earth…'

'You only think?' Zara reprimanded him. 'Then I shall have to convince you…' But, before she could make good her threat, Shahin moved on top of her and, pressing her into the rug, he took her again.

* * *

The Ruby Fort was filled with light as Zara descended the central staircase flanked by Lambert and Gideon. They worked for her now, having taken on the responsibility of marketing her work to a wider audience, as well as directing all their wealthy art buff friends to the magnificent new gallery she had created in Zaddara. All the proceeds from the sale of her images were directed into her charities, and all the proceeds from her gallery in Zaddara went to support the many causes there, for which she and Shahin had taken on joint responsibility.

Shahin stood waiting for her now, his dark eyes burning with love as he stared up at her. Dressed in all the splendour of his rank, he was a formidable, awe-inspiring sight—to everyone but her, Zara mused, trying, but not quite succeeding, to keep the smile from her lips. It was a look only they could share, and only they could interpret. It was a look that spoke of secrets between them, of intimacy and mischief and pleasure. It reminded her that now she had unlocked the door for him, they were both free.

She had protested when he had invaded her room earlier as she was being dressed for the ceremony, and his answer as always had been to dismiss the servants…

'But my hair,' she had protested weakly, as he'd eased the gossamer folds of silk over her head.

'Can be redone,' Shahin had reminded her, sweeping her into his arms.

And then later, when he had shown her the contents of the small velvet box he had with him, she had gasped, 'What is it?'

'Well, it's big, bright and sparkly,' Shahin observed. 'You tell me.'

'And cost the gross national product of which country?' Zara teased him back. 'It's incredible,' she said, reverently touching her fingertip to the huge cushion-cut diamond. 'But do I lay my head on it, or rest my chin on it?'

'You wear it on your finger,' Shahin said, flashing her a mock reproving glance. 'Like this…' Taking the ring out of the box, he placed it on her wedding finger.

'But I didn't…'

'What?' he prompted. 'Expect it? Ask for it? All the more reason for me to give it to you…'

'Will I be able to lift my hand while I'm wearing it?' She opened her eyes very wide.

'I'm sure that should be possible. Shall we have a trial run?' Shahin suggested wickedly.

'It seems you're right,' she said happily, reaching for him…

And now this, the full pomp and ceremony of a royal wedding at the Ruby Fort—after a scant fifteen minutes in which she'd had to shower, rearrange her hair and throw on the most fabulous wedding dress before racing down the endless palace corridors with her attendants in hot pursuit.

She didn't have any relatives to stand up for her and didn't even know half the people, but none of that was important because there was only one person who mattered and he was waiting for her at the foot of the stairs.

Catching hold of her hands, Shahin drew her close, ignoring the whispered words of his aide-de-camp. The man had laid out a very detailed wedding plan, telling him exactly how he should proceed. No Sheikh of Zaddara had ever defied tradition before, or had even wed in public before… But then no Sheikh of Zaddara had ever married his ward before, Shahin reflected, a muscle working in his jaw as he thought about the special treats he had in store for Zara at the desert encampment, where they would be spending their honeymoon.

She'd had no experience of small, thoughtful gifts given to her by someone who loved her as deeply as he did, but all that was about to change. Her life would be transformed... He couldn't wait to see her face when she walked into the privacy of their bridal suite. Would she like the chest of fabulous jewels best, or the full selection of scents and beauty products waiting for her in the bathroom? Perhaps it would be the racks of designer clothes in the dressing room, or possibly the feast he had ordered to surprise her. He'd had the very best chefs and pâtissières flown in from Vienna and Milan to cater for her every whim.

He already knew the answer, Shahin realised, amused to hear a gasp go up as he kissed his bride on the lips. They liked each other, loved each other and enjoyed each other more than anything else the world had to offer them.

'So you do dare to kiss me in public,' she whispered so that only he could hear.

'You should know better than to dare me...' It had been one of her demands for compensation when he had forced his way into her suite of rooms while she had been dressing earlier—and a challenge he had found no difficulty in accepting, or in making good. 'Did you ever doubt me?'

'Never,' Zara admitted, fixing her love-bright eyes on him.

'Shall we?' he invited, taking her soft pale hand in his. 'We mustn't keep our wedding guests waiting,' he reminded her, leading her forward into the light.

* * *

Zara couldn't wait to be rid of the ceremonial guard who had formed behind them. The limousine had taken them as far as the edge of the desert, where Shahin's Jeep was waiting, and now he was going to drive them to his luxury encampment beside the oasis. No guards, no protocol… Heaven. There would just be a skeleton staff to care for them—and this was a new tradition, Shahin had informed her, that would have to be strictly observed every couple of months.

'And for at least a week each time,' Zara had suggested.

'For at least three days and three nights,' Shahin had teased her, reminding her of the pact that had been made when they had first met.

'Must they march with us to the Jeep?' Zara protested, glancing up at Shahin. 'I can't keep in step.'

'You don't have to keep in step,' he reminded her. 'It's up to them to keep in step with you…'

'That only makes me feel worse. And—'

'And?'

'Well, if they're the royal guard, sworn to protect your person with their life, and they all have to march behind you—'

'Yes?'

'What if someone shoots you from the front?'

'Good point,' he murmured dryly. 'I'll have the royal protection programme placed on your desk on Monday morning—'

'I have other plans for Monday morning…'

'I'm relieved to hear it,' He reached across her before any of his men had the chance to open the passenger door of the Jeep for her. 'Now, get in. I'm in a hurry.'

For once she didn't feel like arguing with him.

* * *

He hadn't expected her to burst into tears.

'Shahin, I can't wear all this…'

'Not all at once,' he agreed mildly, enjoying the sight of her holding armfuls of precious jewels up to the light. 'That would be a gross abuse of good taste.'

'You know what I mean… And don't tease me. I'm serious. I've brought you so little—'

'So little? You call the most marvellous images of my country so little? You call your energy to change things, including me, so little? You call love, laughter and a wonderful future so little? You're right,' he said finally, pretending to frown, 'I have every reason to be dissatisfied…'

'Shahin,' Zara reprimanded him softly, brushing the inky locks of hair from his eyes. 'You have to stop teasing me—'

'Not sure I can…'

'But there is one more thing…' She let the jewels slide back inside the casket.

'What is it?' he asked, reclining back on the silken cushions with his hands folded behind his head. He loved just looking at her, filling his eyes with her… He would never tire of it. It was enough for him. It was the only gift on earth he desired.

'I'm not sure if this strictly qualifies as a gift, or if you'll think I'm—'

'Zara…what are you trying to say?' he drawled, noticing she had begun to wring her hands with anxiety.

'This…'

Coming to lie beside him, she placed his hand on her belly.

'What are you telling me?' He searched her eyes.

'I think you know, Shahin…' Pressing her lips together, she waited.

'You mean? Oh, my darling…' Kissing her, Shahin knew instantly and couldn't understand why it hadn't registered before. She even tasted different—warmer, sweeter, full of femininity…and impending motherhood. 'You've made me the happiest man on earth… So why are you crying?'

'I'm overwhelmed by everything you've given me… What?' she asked, staring at the box of tissues Shahin handed her.

'You'd better arm yourself with another wad of tissues in that case, before you read this,' he suggested dryly, handing her an envelope.

'What is it?'

'Your wedding present…'

'But you've already given me too much…'

'And you've given me the greatest gift of all, which is your love. Now, open the envelope.'

Drawing the single sheet of paper out of the thick vellum envelope, Zara read the document through carefully. Shaking her head in disbelief, she read it through again. '"The breeding programme I've set up in Zaddara in your name…"' Pausing, she gazed at Shahin, then, reading out loud, she continued, '"Gazelles, Arabian oryx and other rare creatures… As patron you will be expected to take a very keen interest. I hope you won't find your duties too onerous…" Oh, Shahin…' Leaping up, she flung herself into his arms. 'I love you so much.'

'No more than I love you, my Adara…'

'I don't think you can call me that any longer,' she reminded him.

'Perhaps not…' Shahin's lips pressed down as he pretended to think about it. 'No, your name is Zara, which in

Greek means "bright as the dawn". You came to me with the dawn, and now—'

'You can't get rid of me?'

'You just spoiled a very romantic moment,' Shahin murmured, nuzzling his stubble against her neck in the way he knew she loved.

'Don't worry,' Zara murmured, tracing the planes of his face with her fingers. 'There are going to be plenty more opportunities for you to practice your new found romancing skills…'

'As there will be for you to practice your new skills,' Shahin promised Zara, tumbling her on to her back.

'For ever?' she murmured against his mouth.

'Oh, a lot longer that that, I should think,' Shahin whispered, silencing his beloved wife with a kiss.

FREE

4 BOOKS AND A SURPRISE GIFT!

We would like to take this opportunity to thank you for reading this Mills & Boon® book by offering you the chance to take FOUR more specially selected titles from the Modern Romance™ series absolutely FREE! We're also making this offer to introduce you to the benefits of the Mills & Boon® Reader Service™—

- ★ **FREE home delivery**
- ★ **FREE gifts and competitions**
- ★ **FREE monthly Newsletter**
- ★ **Books available before they're in the shops**
- ★ **Exclusive Reader Service offers**

Accepting these FREE books and gift places you under no obligation to buy; you may cancel at any time, even after receiving your free shipment. Simply complete your details below and return the entire page to the address below. You don't even need a stamp!

YES! Please send me 4 free Modern Romance books and a surprise gift. I understand that unless you hear from me, I will receive 6 superb new titles every month for just £2.80 each, postage and packing free. I am under no obligation to purchase any books and may cancel my subscription at any time. The free books and gift will be mine to keep in any case.

P6ZEE

Ms/Mrs/Miss/Mr.................................Initials ....
                                                                    BLOCK CAPITALS PLEASE
Surname ....
Address ....

....

....Postcode ....

Send this whole page to:
The Reader Service, FREEPOST CN81, Croydon, CR9 3WZ